How to Make a Zombie

a Zombie

"War of the Servers."

Jose Jaime Herrera

iUniverse, Inc.
Bloomington

HOW TO MAKE A ZOMBIE
"WAR OF THE SERVERS."

iUniverse books may be ordered through booksellers or by contacting:

iUniverse
1663 Liberty Drive
Bloomington, IN 47403
www.iuniverse.com
1-800-Authors (1-800-288-4677)

Because of the dynamic nature of the Internet, any web addresses or links contained in this book may have changed since publication and may no longer be valid. The views expressed in this work are solely those of the author and do not necessarily reflect the views of the publisher, and the publisher hereby disclaims any responsibility for them.

Any people depicted in stock imagery provided by Thinkstock are models, and such images are being used for illustrative purposes only.

Certain stock imagery © Thinkstock.

ISBN: 978-1-4759-8514-6 (sc)
ISBN: 978-1-4759-8516-0 (hc)
ISBN: 978-1-4759-8515-3 (e)

Library of Congress Control Number: 2013906353

Printed in the United States of America

iUniverse rev. date: 4/9/2013

ABOUT THE AUTHOR

We all know these are supposed to be in the third person, but it's about me, so I'm writing the damn thing the way I see fit. No changes.

I was born on November 18, 1987, to Denise Garcia and Hector Jaime Herrera of Kingsville, Texas. I have a twin brother, Hector Caesar Herrera; an older sister, Soliel Leigh Pilgrim (deceased); another sister, Elasha Leigh Pilgrim; and a little brother, Juan Diego Herrera (deceased).

My twin brother and I joined the military shortly after high school in 2006, as did most of our friends. He went into the marines as I went into the army, where I still am today. I deployed to Afghanistan in October 2011, and I have had the time of my life. I have read twenty-eight books there, and I am an avionic mechanic. Aircraft are reliable when deployed but break more easily stateside.

A few months after I deployed in 2010, I heard an apocalyptic song and thought, *Damn, that is a hell of a song. I want to write a book.* So I did. I started this book, but downrange I started another before turning back to this book. I felt I should write the backstory before I started to write about the future.

I have already written a book of three morbid stories. The longest one falls into the backstory; the others are in the present time. I will publish them when I find them. I'm currently working on the second installment of the *War of the Servers* series. *Servers* is the second book. It will be out shortly after this one, and I will then work on the third book of the series. Then I can go back to the one I started downrange and continue the saga.

This is my first book, so bear with me on it. I wrote a book because I want to entertain folks with a story line I have had in the works since I graduated high school. So enjoy, and look for the other books in the *War of the Servers* series: *How to Make a Zombie*, *Servers*, *War of the Servers*, and *The Four Emperors*. ☺

Prologue

Life is so simple for us we wake up, comb our hair brush our teeth and if we are lucky we wake up in time to catch the morning commute. We have become a conformist species reliable on technology to cook our food, wash our clothes even make sleeping outdoors like we took a piece of home with us.

But what happens if our norms are taken away from us in a blink of an eye. In truth we can speculate all we want right books make TV shows of men and women trying just to survive.

It is a great idea to see man turn from civilize to an animal in one night. More notorious then out forefathers who founded civilizations. But we will never know how it will turn out will we; we are a species of little interest to go extinct. We are big, we are to smart, and we are to strong that we even cause ourselves damage just opening a jar of our favorite jam.

We are no one special we have too many delusions on destiny, we make stories paint into the sands, while others take it by on foot. But what if our destiny was already written for us, to die out no matter how we try to survive. Could you be do brave to try to save it, even if it takes you own life. If you go the world doesn't stop spinning and flowers keep blooming.

One man cannot do it alone even with enough weapons or friends by his side. It alone most come from determination. The blood on your knuckles and sweat on your brow.

Being so this is a story of just that a story of a young man Hera Kila' Ka. He's just like every man and women; weak and uncertain on how life will take him. Only a simple event can change his destiny and those around him. And with his careless attitude and childlike sense of adventure he will find out why his world and worlds of the Milky Way just up and died one morning.

Enjoy and keep reading the next books, you never know the world might just end.

CHAPTER 1

Ad' Drin, August 22, 3577, 2056 Hours

Hera looked up to the night sky. The lime-green haze slowly changed into crimson red, as it had every night for two years now. The calamity destroyed the first human empire and brought it to ashes under a shower of Lime-Green Stew. All that remained was anarchy: decaying city-states and occupied bands of survivors, slowly watching Ad' Drin die.

Death came in lime-green clouds that exploded into life with four small ships on every human world, in the confederacy as well as arc worlds. This unique energy fell in tendrils, touching random spots on the planet. All it touched fell dead, rotted, or in most cases changed life, turning into mutants or bringing the dead to life.

Hera picked at a small cut on his right forearm. He gazed back at the small city, one of the few remaining on the south end of the continent. A small lime-green cloud sat over the ruined city. Hera could see small lines begin to condense in

1

the cloud. "Tendrils need to hurry. They don't have much time."

Hera was a young man, barely nineteen now. He was six foot two, with skin darkened by the sun, and messy black hair and red highlights.

Hera came up to the gates of the small city, catching his breath. He began to speak. "You need to warn the people of this city. Tendrils are about to fall."

One of two guards approached Hera, yelling at him. "Piss off, boy. The city gates are closed. Come back in the morning."

"Damn it, you, the Lime- Green cloud is going to fall y'all need to warn someone or people will die."

"That cloud has been lingering for weeks. If it was going to fall, it would have by now!"

"Beat it, kid!"

The man raised his weapon to scare Hera away but quickly fell to his knees. Hera punched the man in his lower jaw. The second man jumped from the barrier. Hera had him on the ground before the man realized what happened. The small black sword opened, exposing a barrel. "Tell whoever in charge they need to release everyone. Tendrils are about to fall. Do ya get me?"

Hera ran to the city as sirens were being alarmed. He began to make his way to the center of the city. His goal was to help people escape. He would stay to the last minute. Hera stopped at the sound of singing. "Fucking Christians, no imaginary being is going to save you." Hera raced to the music. A large church dominated the street.

The secular wars unified humans and gave birth to Coelum Simia, a new race of man, much stronger than their predecessors and brought by genetic tapering and exotic climates. Each was capable of doing superhuman feats of strength; these humans had more animal-like stances and movements. Children of the gods waged war with secular simians to purge them from the planet. They were blamed for the destruction of the Earth's ecology, disease, and causing needless deaths. But seculars outnumbered religious three to one, and the war was lost.

People's singing in the church turned into screams as Hera blasted the doors open. "Everyone, you need to evacuate the city. Tendrils are about to fall."

"We know, my dear boy, that's why we are here. We are ready to return to god."

"You can't believe that, sir."

"How many churches, young man, have you barged in, asking for people to go with you, and how many left in your hands?"

"Actually this is my first. I usually let y'all die."

"We are here to give our souls to the savior, son. All we ask for is peace."

"And you shall have it. Sorry for interrupting your sermon, sir."

"All is forgiven."

"If anyone wants to come with me, you shall,

but I'm going to leave now." Hera lowered his weapon and went for the door.

"Wait." Hera turned to see a young girl, who was maybe seventeen, with tears in her eyes. She had pale skin and orange hair with blue highlights.

"Star, if you go with him, you abandon god."

"No, Mum, I don't. He's not my god. He's yours."

Star took off after Hera, her mother screaming for her behind her. Hera was waiting for her outside the church. "Let's go."

Star had trouble keeping up with Hera's pace, but she did her best. Chaos roamed the street, as it was every man for himself.

"Come on, we are almost to the city gates." Hera grabbed the girl's arm and hauled her through the crowd.

Star turned her head to look behind her. Tendrils began to touch down. Long arms of lime-green exotic radiation wrapped itself around every object it touched. Then with no effort crushed building to their foundations. Blue lighting shot from the arms, striking people in the streets or blanketing them in lime-green haze. Star and Hera made it out of the doomed city. Hera ran for the crowd of people.

"Hey, can I have everyone's attention? We need to keep moving. The cloud has killed the city, but it will not remain such for long. There's a safe zone about ten miles south of here. I suggest you get moving or die this night. That is where I'm going. Please, everyone, follow behind me."

Hi' Ko Safe Zone, August 23, 3577, 0410 Hours

Hera was in front of the crowd, leading them to safety. "What's your name, girl?" Hera asked.

"Star," the girl said, turning her tired eyes to him. "Star Cassidy."

"Star Cassidy sounds like a cowboy," Hera said.

"What is your name?" Star asked.

"Hera Kila' Ka."

"Hera, I believe that first I heard that name on a man before."

Hera laughed. "My parents were hippies."

"Oh, I'm sorry, Hera," Star replied.

"Mum's not dead, nor is my father or younger sister. They are all alive in T' ne."

"Okay, sorry, I guess. What is it you exactly do around here in the wasteland?"

It took some time before Hera answered, "I roamed the waste to help survivors, tell them where they need to go to find T' ne. Food, safety, weapons, rights, and a clean slate are waiting for them there."

"I take it that's where we are not going, is it?" Star asked Hera.

Hera pulled out a cigarette from an unused ammo pouch. "Nope, we are not. T' ne is over two hundred miles away, and I am no babysitter. I'm taking everyone to Hi' Ko. There you have a place to live and work. If not, you'll leave with clothes on your back. Speaking of which, we are here." Hera ran in front of the crowd, stopping them. "If everyone would wait here for a minute, thank you." Hera walked to the gate of Hi' Ko City. He was approached by men in hazmat gear.

Star tried to hear what they were talking about. She tried to get closer through the crowd but was stopped by one of the men in biohazard gear. "Hey, what the hell! Let go of me!"

"Sorry, ma'am, it's protocol."

"Hera, please help me!"

"No, you all are not my problem anymore!"

"Hera!"

Star and other survivors were taken by the men in hazmat, through the city gates. Other men were in civilian attire. They opened a giant hangar door. Star began to cry. She knew what would happen now. "What are y'all doing to me?" The men stayed silent. "Answer me, damn you!"

Star was thrown into the wall. The men began to search her for valuables, as they did with everyone who made their way to Hi' Ko. "No, leave me alone. Stop it, please." Star was on the cold cement, hugging her body. The men began to throw delousing power and other chemicals on her. "What the fuck! This burns!" Star tried to clear her eyes but was hosed down by water.

She was immediately thrown to her knees. The water was colder than she had ever felt before. Gasping for air, she still tried to yell, "Stop."

The water stopped as soon as it had started. Star was then drugged over to a chair in a room. Two female nurses approached her and began to examine her.

One of the nurses pulled out a tablet and began to ask Star questions. "What is your name?"

"Star. Star Cassidy."

"Age?"

"Seventeen."

"Any known diseases?"

"None. I was fine until y'all hosed me down with ice water."

"Just a precaution, that is all. Here are your paperwork, key to your trailer, and directions. A new life has been set for you."

"Well, it's a good thing I took a bath." Star took the envelope from the women, and they walked away. Star walked to a small box. Clothes that were roughly her size were packed inside the box.

Hi' Ko Safe Zone, September 27, 3577, 0934 Hours

Star had a job now with everyone who came to Hi' Ko. She worked at a small restaurant as a waitress. It was not a life she wanted, but she couldn't complain. Her boss was an old man, toughened by hard labor but with the heart of a saint. Star took some drinks to some customers.

"Hey there, little girl." One of the men came up to her.

"Excuse me, sir, but I have to get back to work or get fired."

"No, no, I just want to talk, that's all." The man grabbed Star and threw her on the table.

"Hey, assholes, piss off!"

His friends began to laugh at Star. "Gets them every time!"

"No, leave me alone." Star looked around for anyone to help, but no one would help her. They all went about their own business.

"I would leave her alone, peanut dick, if I were you." Hera was standing in the doorway, puffing on a crush cigarette.

"Piss off, boy. This is none of your business!" the man holding Star called out.

Hera looked down at his cigarette. "You know what really pisses me off? When I can't enjoy a smoke. I guess I will have to light another one when you're all dead."

"I said fuck off, you—" The man's sentence was cut off. Hera's sword sliced the top half of his head.

"You son of bitch!" one of the man's friends called out. He drew his weapon, sending orange bolts of plasma toward Hera. Hera spun his sword, parrying the plasma to the other friend and killing him before he could react.

The man kept firing in vain, as Hera blocked every blast. "You're dead." Hera parried the man last bolt of plasma unto his weapon. He was blinded by a flash. When he opened his eyes, Hera was standing next to him. He raised his arm only to realize it had been cut off by Hera.

"You—" The man's body fell limp as Hera apparently did more damage the instant the man was blinded by his own fire.

Hera cleaned his small sword with some paper towels and sat down. He pulled out another cigarette from his pack and lit it. Hera took a long drag and looked up at Star. "I'll take a sweet tea and your lunch special."

"It's canned soup," Star replied, staring blankly at Hera.

"Well, that will be fine. I'll take some crackers to go with it."

Star fainted on the table near him, collapsing.

"Hey, wake up. My soup is getting cold."

1656 Hours

Star's boss came to Star. "You can go home now. I'll see you at eight in the morning."

"Sir, what do you know about Hera Kila' Ka?"

"You can call me Peter, dear."

"Well, Peter, what do you know?"

"Hera Kila' Ka is in a world of his own. Not much is known about him. He comes and goes as he pleases. He's rude but kind. He has helped many people here and elsewhere. If not for Hera, half of this city would be dead. Hera's main goal is to find people in the waste and show them where T' ne is, so they can start a new life."

"Doesn't he escort people there, Peter?"

"No, he just shows them the way to the islands."

"Fuck, I was hoping I could have him take me there. I know I have only been here a month, but it's time for me to leave!"

"Then why don't you ask him yourself, Star. I'm having a get-together tonight, and he will be here."

Star jumped up with excitement. "Yes, I will ask him. Thank you, Peter."

"No problem, dear. Be here at seven."

1910 Hours

Star was one of the first guests to arrive at Peter's house, so she waited for Hera to arrive. Guest after guest came, but no Hera. *Damn it, when are you coming?* Star looked impatiently at her watch. She quickly looked around to see if he had come in. *Nope, not in that corner, or that one. Fuck.*

"Looking for me?"

"Shit!" Star jumped from her seat to find Hera standing behind her. "Hi, I guess."

Hera turned around and sat in a chair in the kitchen. Star pulled out a cigarette and slowly lit it. "Never too young to start, huh?"

How am I going to ask him? He just turns away from me. He's a dick. No, I will get him to take me to T' ne.

"Are you done talking in your head and ready to say what you want out loud?"

Star's hair flew as she turned her head to Hera. "Yes, I am, Hera. I am ready. I want you to escort me to T' ne!"

The whole room grew quiet and looked at Star.

"No!"

"No? Why not?"

"Because I only show people the way. I don't

escort them there. I won't be responsible for simian or alien life, for that matter."

"Really, you're so willing to save lives but will not take responsibility for helping them. You're just like any other typical asshole that the calamity created."

"I brought you here, Star. I saved your life. What more do you want? Shit, girls at least put out before they ask me for something."

The whole room began to laugh at Hera's remark. "I can't kick you out, since this is not my house, but you know where the door is." Hera went to take another shot from his bottle but crashed through the table.

"Holy shit," Peter said. "Those chairs aren't cheap!"

"Sorry, Peter, but I planned it from the start."

Star reached in her bag for duct tape and proceeded to tape up Hera. "You plan to take advantage of him?"

"No, not that. I just want to talk to him while he's defenseless. That's all."

Star leaned over Hera, who was tied to a tree in Peter's backyard, and poured water on him.

"Fuck no, Mommy, I didn't do it. I swear!"

"I'm not going to hurt you, Jesus fuck tits. I just want to talk."

Hera tried to wiggle free from the tape but instantly stopped when he realized it was fruitless. "I already said no, Star."

"Can't I just follow you on this journey, and I'll

just jump on a boat to T' ne? I mean, you must go see your family, right?"

"No, no, I don't. I've been out here for two years but not without contact. I can't have that on my conscience if you get hurt. You're better off here than out there. Wait, what are you doing?"

Star sat on top of Hera and began to make out with him. Hera moved himself out of Star kiss. "Silly girl, playing with my heart won't make me take you there."

"I'm not fucking you."

"Ah, get your hands off my no, no square!"

"What no no square, Hera are you some kind of wussy, Hera?"

"No, I'm not a little bitch."

Star leaned her head toward Hera. "Well then, Hera?"

Hera looked at all the duct tape around him, and then he looked up at the sky for a moment. "We leave in two days!" Hera said to stop her.

Star jumped off Hera in excitement. "Really? You really mean it?"

"Yes, I do, even though it goes against my better judgment. I will allow you to come with me. Now untie me, woman!" Hera looked around, but Star had gone inside. "Really, well, at least she left me her beer." Hera tried to free his arm to grab Star's beverage, but to no avail. "Damn!"

Hi' Ko Safe Zone, September 29, 3577, 0934 Hours

Hera had his gear ready for his trip, but all he needed was Star. He gazed at the streets. Nothing but people with no hope clouded the city streets. *Can't save them all. Not my job.*

"Hera, right behind you."

"Shit, woman."

"Sorry, but I've been here for some time now."

"Damn it, you should have said something. Creeping on me—that's scary."

Star smiled. "What?"

"Nothing, I'm ready to go, Hera."

"All right, I got something for you." Hera pulled two small pistols out of a brown bag. "They are semi-auto, but if you fire both in unison, they will fire automatic. You just need to find the rhythm."

"Thank you, Hera. They're new. Did they cost you a lot of money?"

"Yes, they did, but that doesn't matter. They will keep you safe."

"Thank you, Hera."

"You're welcome, Star."

CHAPTER 2

Wasteland, October 3, 3577, 0431 Hours

Star pulled off her boots. She and Hera had stopped for a break, since the smell of rain masked their odor. Star gazed under her big toe. "Ouch! A large blister, damn. Should I pop it?"

"If you want to, it will heal faster."

Hera walked over to the body of a zombie they had just killed and began to smell it.

"Hurry up. It seems they are all doing it now."

"Doing what now?"

"Mutants or zombies release a pheromone. It smells just like they do—a rotting bag of meat—but women can't smell it."

"Oh, okay."

"I don't know why women can't smell the pheromone, but now we can't stay here. So remember that if you kill one, you invite others to the tea party."

Wasteland, October 7, 3577, 1756 Hours

Hera and Star looked around at the city.

Thousands of dead and mutated simians and Kopi stood in their path.

"Ready, Star?"

"Is that a question or a statement?"

"Whatever you want!"

Star looked one last time at the city. "Let's go."

Hera jumped onto a semitrailer that was turned over. "Kill the ones only in your path, and jump from car to car."

Hera ran on all fours. It was the easiest way for simians to trek a long distance in a short amount of time. Hera stood on two legs to deal with the dead in his path. Star jumped into the air, firing her weapon and shooting the dead before she landed. Pink bolts of plasma made contact with the dead, sending white flashes that destroyed their flesh. She landed on a small trunk, performed a windmill, and tripped on a mutated Kopi that launched for her.

Hera's sword met the heads of the dead. The small sword easily sliced and mutated flesh.

Satisfied with the carnage, Hera sprinted to a light pole, jumped to the fixture, and grabbed on, tossing himself a good fifty feet into the air. Hera reached for his Magnum pistols. Large orange bolts buried themselves in mutants, leaving them burning piles of devastated flesh.

Hera landed on the Ad' Drin, shattering asphalt under him. He turned his head to Star. He flipped in the air, sending precise shots into dead beings. Star landed to Hera's right. Hera pointed to a building that read "Ne'Ka Subway Station." She mirrored Hera: blade in the left hand and firearm in the right.

Hera fired a series of shots. Each one perforated their targets with enough energy to destroy whatever lay behind them. A mutant jumped for Hera. He laughed as he sliced the mutant, using it as a stepping stool to gain air. Hera then landed, sticking his Magnum into the head of a zombie. He fired without giving a second thought. The dead man exploded from the powerful weapon. The bolt continued as a stray, striking a car's reactor.

The car explosion cleared everything in his path. *"Not what I was going for, but pretty fucking awesome nevertheless."*

Star spun over a mutated woman. Time slowed down as her weapon barrel lined up with the mutant head. Pink plasma buried itself into her. She landed on all fours, looking forward at the sea of dead. "Shit, yeah!" Star sheathed her blade and went for the sister weapon. She raised both pistols and began to fire.

She found the weapons' rhythm, allowing them to fire automatically. A burst of pink plasma struck targets as she ran. Bodies began to fall. Even if they didn't die, they fell in ruin. There was one large mutant in their path.

"Mine!" Hera called out. Hera's right fist glowed red as energy spun around his fist.

The large mutant stretched its long arms. One was still simian; the other was a large claw that dripped yellow pus. Hera fired his weapon before landing. The plasma bolt severed the claw arm. The mutant buckled in pain as Hera landed in front of the twisted being. He placed his hand on the mutant chest. Tentacles burst from the mutant body and wrapped around Hera's arm.

"How do you feel about sexual assault, boy?"

The mutant body erupted in white energy. The energy blast continued as a wave of energy, clearing everything in fifty yards.

"We need to make a dead sprint to the building. It's only a hundred yards away."

Hera ran on all fours, faster than if he was on two legs. Star followed him. Hera cleared the path of dead bodies, ramming them down. Star did the best she could to keep up. The subway station was only meters away now.

"Jump, Star."

Hera leaped into the air like a lemur, landing on top of the building with ease. Star landed on the roof, half on and half off, but Hera helped her up. "Fuck, I'm tired," Star said, rolling on her back. Hera sat with his legs crossed, looking at the ruined street. The cars on fire began to explode as the reactors were damaged. He looked in relief as the whole street went up in flames, clearing away the zombies and mutants.

Red mushroom clouds climbed into the sky. It was a relief to his eyes as the dead ran in flames.

"Let's get inside, Star, and call it a night."

Ne'Ka Subway Station, 1923 Hours

"It's okay if you use the sink for a bird path, Star," Hera said, pointing to the sink in the restroom.

Star walked to the sink and took off her shirt. She lathered a washcloth with soap and water. "Hera, you don't have to look."

"Sorry!" Hera said, looking away as she dropped her pants. He slowly turned back to her, noticing she was once bit a long time ago.

"You're immune, like myself." Star looked down at her stomach. A small scar was visible. She turned to Hera, who displayed his own scar on his arm.

"My mother and I are from a small town. Then the calamity happened, and we were stuck. We made the decision to leave our home. There was nothing left. We had only been away for two hours when I was bitten. So my mother hid me in a store, and I began to grow sick, screaming in pain, hallucinating."

Star put on a clean shirt and walked over to Hera. "Four men came in and found me, but they wouldn't kill me. They knew I was immune because they were, as well. They protected my mother and me until I got better. They said they could take us to safety, so for two weeks we tagged along until we came to the gates of the city I was in, where you saved me. I turned around to thank them, but they were gone, like they were never there to begin with."

A small tear rolled from Star's eye. "Tell me about you, Hera."

Hera had walked over to the sink and began to clean himself.

"My father trained my friends and me in combat since we were ten years of age. My goal was to be in the Light Fleet. I wanted to see more alien planets conquer them, like our ancestors did for over a thousand years. I became a grunt, my friend a pilot, and the other a medic. We made our family proud. They threw a large party for us on T' ne. I was happy I got selected to go to the Order of Light, but the next day those ships came. My parents didn't want me to go. I didn't have a unit, and they wouldn't miss me, my father said. But I left anyway. I made my way to Ne'Ka by plane and joined the unit station here."

Hera walked back to the bed made of blankets. "It was not war. The outbreak made faster by falling radiation destroyed my reason to fight. There was no point. It was genocide, not war, and it was lost the instant it happened. I got bit and made my way to this station. I lay on this floor, crying until I fell asleep. And when I woke I was not sick anymore. I was cured. There were no black bumps on my arm or groin, as is the sign of Zombism. I want back outside. There was nothing but a silent city with only flames in the horizon. I walked for the better part of the day, looking for someone from my unit or at least a civilian, but no one was there.

"I realized I was not armed, so I picked up a weapon from a dead soldier and looked back at the burning city and said to myself, 'I can't get infected. I have nothing to lose.' I roamed

20

the newly formed wasteland for a good month, avoiding all contact with survivors. I came across what was left of a military TOC and found a tablet. I turned on the tablet and tuned it to my father's frequency. I got ahold of him very easily. He said to me, 'I got a mission for you.' I've been out here ever since for two years, talking through him with the same tablet, helping him gather medicine and telling people where to go to find T' ne.

"Star, do you know how you became infected?"

"Actually I never put any thought into it. I always presumed it was the lime-green energy."

Hera pulled out a cigarette and handed the pack to Star. "That's one way to become infected. The radiation kills you, but the damage touches your DNA. It reorganizes in your body. Then slowly but surely parasites form. These parasites bring you back to life as a zombie or mutant, and if bit by one they spread into you. The parasites have collective intelligence, riding the host like a car. Somewhat they are not in full control."

"Who would do this to us?"

Hera finally lit his cigarette and then handed the lighter to Star. "I don't know, but from what I see, this is how they say hello."

"That's not a good way to make friends," Star said, releasing her drag.

Hera laughed for a second. "We are no different. We left Earth with a hole in our heart that burned the solar systems. We came across worlds devouring all native life forms and then seeding it with ours.

And to top it off, if we came across a world with sentient life, we destroyed it. Even if those races were in our empire or met their first alien life for the first time, we said, 'Hello, you can join us, but first we need to kick your ass.'"

Hera took another drag. "They are doing the same with us, but they don't blacken the skies like us; they radiate and cause new life to form. Their own life is what I get from it, but I was an infantryman, not a xenobiologist." Hera stood up and walked out of the room. He didn't want to talk anymore for the moment. He walked into the next room. It had a fridge with power still running. "Sweet, still here." Hera walked back to Star and threw her an ice cream bar.

"Really I haven't had one for two years." Star opened the wrapper, biting the bar as if she was late to get somewhere.

"Slow down," Hera said, biting into his. "You don't want to get brain freeze, do ya?"

"Thank you, Hera. Besides the death run, this made my day."

"Well, enjoy, because they are now extinct."

"Where are we heading from here, Hera?"

"We are heading to Nil' Ka to see if they can give you a flight home, but first we need to stop outside of town."

"What is there for us?"

"Not us. It is for my father's anti-radiation medicine. It's in a small hospital outside of town. It is for the pre-stages of Zombism. Basically people are exposed to small doses of the radiation at all times and are slowly becoming infected."

"And it will help reverse the damage?" Star added.

"The only known cure, but you have to catch it when symptoms show before they get too serious. Or it's a bolt of plasma to your head."

"Hey, why don't we take a flying car to T' ne?"

"Flying cars only came out a few months before the calamity, even though they are DNA locked to the owner. If you want to find the mutated owner, be my guest."

"They have to help me get to T' ne then. How far are we from Nil' Ka, Hera?"

"One hundred and twenty-one miles, but I'll get you there. I promise I will not let you down."

"Thank you, Hera."

"Let's get some sleep. We need to be rested for our little hike ahead. It will take two days, but at least we are heading in the right direction."

Ne'Ka City Outskirts, October 9, 3577, 1101 Hours

Hera jumped onto a burned car and pointed to a lone building in a field. "Right there, that's the hospital."

Star gazed at the lone building. One of the floors was still burning; smoke was rising to meet the clouds.

"Hey, Hera, can we eat lunch under that bridge?"

"Well, it looks safe enough. We should just be very quiet." Hera and Star made a dead sprint to the bridge. Hera stopped right under as Star went to investigate a motor home. Hera looked around and began to sniff the air. "Someone has been cooking here and recently. Star, wait, don't go in there."

Star fell to the ground as a large man kicked the door from the other side. Hera raised his weapon to kill the man.

"I'd drop it if I were you, boy."

Hera dropped his weapon on the cold Ad' Drin and slowly turned to his captor.

"Good boy, now slowly turn on your back."

Hera looked over the two men. One was wearing dog tags like the military personnel wear. "You're deserters, are you?"

"How did you guess that?" asked the man, spitting by Hera's feet.

"Because I too am a dog with no master, just like you."

"Oh, save us the speech on how mugging people has no merit."

"No, he and his little girlfriend are just going to kill you." A man in black fatigues was sitting on top of a motor home.

"Will you shut up, Peshe, and come down here?"

"What's your name, kid?"

"Hera Kila' Ka."

"Well now, Hera, will you hurry up and kill them so we can fight?"

"AL righty then, one second." Hera sliced his

24

captor faster than he could ask what was going on.

The other man beside him raised his weapon, firing at Hera. Hera jumped into the air, spinning his sword. Hera slowly advanced, taunting the man. Blue and white sparks flew off his weapon as he parried the rapid burst of plasma. Hera sent one back at the man, hitting him in the head. Hera turned to the last man standing over Star. "You move, she's—" The last man fell to the ground. Hera stood behind him, cleaning blood off his sword on the man's jacket before he fell.

"Faster than words." Hera walked farther out so he could get a better look at the man in black fatigues. He stood on top of the motor home, using his gun blade like a cane.

"Let me introduce myself. The name is Second Lieutenant Yonin Peshe."

"Wait," Star said to the man, "is that Yonin as in Yo, or Yonin as in Joe?"

"It's Yonin as in Yo."

"That's a good question!" said Hera, looking at Star.

"I knew a Jonin, but I've never heard of Yonin before, so I had to ask."

"Okay, enough with my name. My parents were stoners."

"Yes," said Hera, "we were just about to fight."

"No, no fighting!"

"What? But you said—"

"I know what I said, Hera. I was only joking.

We are not going to fight," said Yonin, closing the blades of his weapon before jumping off the motor home to meet Hera and Star face-to-face. "I just met these guys like two days ago. I was going to investigate the explosions in town. But I felt like I was getting a cold, so when I found these guys I decided to chill with them until I got better."

"And your cold?" Hera asked.

"Allergies," said Yonin, stretching and looking at Star. She gave him a raised eyebrow that said, "Look away."

"Okay, then we are going to the hospital to get some medicine. Do you want to tag along?" asked Hera.

"Sure, be more than happy to. What are you going to get, Hera?"

"We are getting potassium iodine."

"Radiation medicine. What in the hell do you need that for?" asked Yonin.

"It's not for us. It's for my father. Potassium iodine is the only cure for Zombism. Exposure to the tendrils of energy causes infection, and potassium iodine can cure it somewhat. But it only prevents the parasites from forming in a person exposed to the exotic radiation, that's it."

"Okay then, but first did y'all say you were just going to eat lunch? Because I'm starving."

Ne'Ka City Hospital, 1210 Hours

Hera and Yonin cleared the main lobby of zombies. Star followed behind them, targeting the infected they had missed. Yonin drew his sword.

The large blade sliced a mutant straight down the middle. Hera flew over him, lopping off heads before he landed on the ground.

Hera looked around the lobby to see if any more were around. "Clear!" Hera walked to the map. The pharmacy is just down this hall to the left."

"Okay then," Yonin added, "I'm on point."

"Star, follow behind me."

"So what are y'all doing out here in the lovely waste?"

"I'm escorting Star to my father's island of T' ne. Here's a flyer. It tells you how to get there."

Yonin took the flyer and looked it over. He put it in his pocket. "Thank you. Something to consider." Yonin popped his head around the corner. "Looks all clear." He pushed the door open. Nothing jumped out at him. He turned his head to Hera and motioned for him to come.

"Okay, then start looking for small yellow boxes. Star, it's dark in here, so be careful."

"I will, Hera. Does your father want any other medicine?"

"Yes, he does. Antibiotics and prescription medicine. We'll grab what we need first but then get whatever looks important."

Hera walked around the corner, looking at boxes of medicine. He hummed to himself, "Not these shelves."

Hera was thrown backward, screaming, "Zombie doctor, and he's mad because we are going to take medicine without a prescription!"

Hera reached for a drum and smashed the zombie head open.

Yonin and Star ran to Hera. "And you said for me to be careful, huh?"

"It is all good. We have what we came for. These drums have the medicine inside," said Hera, popping a drum open.

"That was very convenient to find what you're looking for so quickly."

"Let's get some other stuff and make our way to the top of the building."

Ne'Ka City Hospital, 1230 Hours

Hera pulled out a tablet and began to call his father. Star and Yonin walked over to Hera to view the tablet. "Hera," said an old man from the tablet.

"Dad, we got the potassium iodine and some other medicines that might be useful."

"We? I thought you traveled alone, Hera."

"Well, Dad, I do, but I promised her I would take her to T' ne, so up till then I'll be accompanied by Star Cassidy. And there's something I want to ask you. Is there any way you can send a ship to come get her?"

"Sorry, Hera, but our resources are limited from fighting the infection on the island. But let me know when you get closer, and I'll see what I can do."

"Thank you, Dad. We are on our way from Nil' Ka. They might be able to help. You can send the drones to get your supplies."

"All right, I'll send some food and ammo with them for you and your guest."

"Okay, Dad, I'm sending the coordinates right now."

"Okay, Hera, could you put the girl on?"

Hera handed the tablet to Star. She grabbed the tablet with hesitation. "Hello," she said, looking at the old man on the other side.

"Hello, Star, I see you are keeping my son occupied." Star laughed a bit, looking at Hera. "What is your height and size, sweetie?"

"Uh, five feet two, 110 pounds. Why, sir, you a cannibal?"

Hera and Yonin laughed at her comment.

"No, dear, I'll have something waiting for you when you arrive."

"Okay, sir, can't wait," Star said, handing Hera his tablet back. "That was random, huh?"

"My dad's a pimp, but in all seriousness he'll have a gift waiting for you, and you will like it."

"Oh, I'm forced to like it."

"Yes, love is forced at home. Our shit should be here by now." Hera pointed to the horizon. Two drones could be made out racing through the clouds. They were carrying nets under their bodies. Hera used the tablet to control their descent. Yonin helped him guide them down. "All right, let's see what my father gave us."

Star picked up a small submachine gun. "I'll take this one, and I've fired this model before."

Hera just loaded his ammo pouches as Yonin took an assault rifle.

1324 Hours

"Hera," Yonin called as they walked up the bridge. They met early. He tossed keys to him.

"Take her home, Hera."

"You're not going to come with us, Yonin?"

"No, but I feel our paths will cross again. I might make my way there. I don't know."

"Thank you, Yonin. The motor home will get us there that much sooner. Let's go, Star."

CHAPTER 3

Nil' Ka City, October 8, 3577, 1643 Hours

Hera and Star weren't far from the hospital now. Lime-green energy hugged the skies over the city, mixing with a hue of the ashen sky.

Star looked over the bridge they were crossing. Some men on motorcycles stopped to kill some mutants, which lined the streets. She knew not to talk to strangers out here, for you might talk to the wrong ones.

She ran back up to Hera, whom she had fallen behind. Hera handed her a cigarette, and they rested on the side of a truck.

Without saying a word, he gazed at the city in the background as a tendril wrapped around a building. Lime-green energy began to constrict the building. Blue lights jumped from building to building, setting fire to the city in the background.

"We build from dust our empire, and in the end it all shall return to dust, blotting out the night sky, hiding evidence that men once played here." Hera flicked his cigarette over the bridge. "Let's go."

Wasteland, Sixty-Seven Miles from Nil' Ka City, October 11, 3577, 0815 Hours

Hera had to take a longer route than he wanted. Streets were lined with lost people picking survivors off the road. Hera plugged in his iPod as Star woke up in the seat next to him. "Morning, sunshine."

"How long was I passed out?"

"About eighteen hours, mama."

"Eighteen hours? Shit, I guess it's my time to drive, huh!"

"We will switch out when we get to the next town." Hera turned on his iPod. He chose a song that fit the situation. "I always want to play this song while driving in the waste."

Star tilted her head. "It sounds apocalyptic. I like it." Star reached over the dash for a cigarette. She lit the cigarette and asked Hera a question. "Where are we, Hera?"

"Near Palis. It's a small town with a large Christian temple. From what I hear, a med station was opened up in the temple as one last-ditch effort to combat the alien invasion."

Star gazed at Hera. His face showed fatigue. "Pull over, Hera. I'll drive from here."

Palis City, 0934 Hours

Hera woke to the sound of the motor home stopping suddenly. "We are here, Hera."

Hera yawned and stretched against the motor home. Star looked at the temple. One large pyramid stood over smaller temples. "Do you think the pyramid has the medicine?"

"I don't know, but the pyramid is hollow with many rooms. We might be here all day."

Hera and Star walked into the pyramid. The doors slid open as they passed. "The temple is solar powered, and I'm surprised that no one set up shop here. This place is safe."

"Damn, son, this place is nice!"

"I think we are in the center of the pyramid, Star. Well, at least from what I heard about this place, the center has a giant fruit garden."

Hera and Star went through another sliding door into a large room and entered the temple garden. Plants grew wild, and vines hugged the walls and every pillar in the center.

"Wow, this place is amazing. Look at all the fruit plants just growing. I wonder if visitors are allowed a taste."

Hera gazed at the ceiling. Plants grew on an obelisk that pierced an opening in the ceiling. "Who would have guessed even at the end of the world plants still bend toward the light?"

"Star," Hera called to her as she picked a fruit off a vine. "The lime-green radiation infects everything living. Hera reached for a small blade to cut the fruit. "See, Star, the fruit doesn't belong to us." Large white parasites danced freely in the air, searching their assailants who damaged their home.

"Are those the parasites that cause infection?"

"Yes, Star, the radiation infects DNA, growing to maturity in hours or days. We are immune to the small black ones, not these—well, maybe these too." Hera sat on the floor. He plucked a parasite from the fruit. The long white worm crawled on the floor. Multiple glowing lime-green eyes searched for a host. Hera cut his finger until blood began to gather at the tip. One drop fell onto the parasite.

"Huh, mmmm." The white worm continued to crawl unfazed. Hera raised his foot to squash the little critter. The parasite began to scream and shake. Its body ruptured, sending orange pus flying. Hera looked at Star with a goofy face. "Let's eat!"

"I guess we are immune to all parasites, so no worries." Star bit into a large blue fruit. Parasites emerged. She plucked one and spit on it. The worm started to scream comically before bursting. "This is fun, Hera." Star dropped the fruit on the ground and followed Hera's eyes. "We were too loud."

Star looked into the center of the room. A large humanoid mutant gazed back. With hollow eyes it stood ten feet tall. Large tentacles touched the ground. The body had multiple distorted faces biting the air.

Yellow gray pus dripped from every face and tentacle. The mutant stared at Hera and Star, waiting its move. "Rotting man."

"What?"

"I'll explain later, Star, but shoot every tentacle you see and all the faces, and when they are all gone, shoot at random on the body."

"Why, Hera? Cannot we just shoot it in the head?"

"No, the corpse is only a shell. The real beast is inside. Now attack."

The rotting man raised his massive arms into the air, releasing a powerful roar that silenced all other noises. Hera and Star leaped into the air only to be brought back by pus-covered tentacles.

Tentacles wrapped around Star, lifting her into the air. They began to draw her to a face on the rotting man's shoulder. The ruined face began to enlarge, releasing more yellow-gray pus-covered tentacles that wrapped themselves around Star.

Hera came out of his daze. Star was already halfway into the mutant body. "Star." Hera flexed his upper body, breaking free from the grasp of the rotting man. He raised his arms and allowed a weapon to materialize in his hands. Hera leaped to the mutant, shattering the Ad' Drin beneath his feet. His weapon sliced into the body of the rotting man, anchoring him on the shoulder.

Hera grabbed Star's legs and tried to pull her free from the rotting man's mouth. The mutant head looked up at him. His eyes met the mutant's as a white burst of energy perforated his left shoulder. Hera fell to the temple floor.

He looked back at the rotting man. Star slid into the mutant's body. Hera's eyes began to tear. "Star."

The mutant raised his right arm and plunged down. Hera caught the massive arm in his left hand with little ease. Hera punched into the mutant and pulled Star from the rotting innards of the rotting man.

She looked up at Hera and vomited on them both. Hera almost lost hold of her as he moved her behind him. The rotting man opened his mouth. Energy lit the room as Hera raised his hand just in time to parry the attack.

Hera looked back up at the rotting man. The majority of the plants in the garden were in flames. "Are you okay, Star?"

"Are you fucking kidding me? I was swallowed by a zombie. Not quite a vacation."

Hera looked back at the mutant as it began to charge. Both Hera and Star fired their weapons. The rotting man lunged forward, unaffected by their attack.

It grabbed Hera and Star, pushing them through marble walls, and continued to ram them through adjacent pillars in the main cathedral. Hera and Star fell to the floor, screaming in pain. The rotting man and its many faces laughed at their injured toys.

The rotting man finally spoke. "I will savor the flesh of the girl. As for you, boy, you will join my collective."

"Star, you see all these balconies and light fixtures? Jump up to them. I have an attack but need time to charge."

"All right, hope it works."

"Me too. I've never tried it. I just learned it."

The rotting man charged Hera and Star, tripping as they jumped into the air. Star hung from a chandelier. She drew her weapon, firing on the rotting man. It stood motionless, laughing.

36

"Hera, it's not working."

"Keep firing, Star. Aim for the tentacles."

The giant mutant's mouth and eyes began to glow white, firing a beam of white energy at Star.

"Shit." Star monkeyed onto a balcony just as the ceiling was incinerated.

Hera's arm was glowing a dark shade of blue. The rotting man turned his head to his direction, firing, and Hera leaped onto a chandelier, firing his Magnum. A bright burst of orange plasma struck the mutant tentacles. The rotting man roared as tentacles on its body burst, freeing black and clear fluid.

Star loaded her weapon's missile launcher. She was thrown back as it fired. Star and Hera waited for the explosion. The rotting man laughed as the missile floated above its head. The missile slowly turned to her and then raced in the direction of Star.

Star jumped from the balcony and onto the cathedral floor. She reached for a weapon on her back. The weapon whined to life as it unfolded, exposing a long blade.

Star jumped into the air, aiming her weapon at the rotting man. The large mutant swatted her and sent her flying into the altar of the cathedral. Hera landed beside Star, firing his Magnum and keeping the rotting man at bay.

"Star, run! My attack is charged. Get as far away as possible."

"What about you, Hera?"

"I'll be fine, Star. I have to get close. I don't want him sending the attack flying back at us. It needs to be point-blank."

Star ran for the ruined wall, hiding behind rubble.

The rotting man slowly turned to him. "Hey."

Hera fired his weapon on the mutant, charging it. The rotting man stopped him, pinning Hera down with its tentacles. Hera freed his arm. A bright ball of energy floated to the rotting man and perforated its chest.

"Oh, shit, I'm too close." Star was thrown out of the cathedral, shaking from the massive explosion. She ran back inside, yelling for Hera through the ashen atmosphere. "Hera, can you hear me?" Star ran into the middle of the room and began to dig through fallen architecture. "Hera, please don't be dead. Please don't." Star jumped back as the debris began to shift.

Hera stood up, covered in dust and blood. He ripped off Star's burned shirt and used it to wipe him clean. He looked back at Star and could see tears in her eyes. He looked away and smiled. "Sorry, didn't think you loved that shirt so much."

Palis City, 1042 Hours

Hera walked out of the shower in the pyramid shower room. Star was on the opposite side of the locker room. "Hera, why did it take us eighteen hours to travel only sixty miles?"

"We were on a dangerous side of the highway. There are lots of men waiting at every bridge or fork in the road, not to mention I got lost for like ten hours."

"Oh, I thought you knew your way around the wasteland, Hera, but at least I'm that much closer to T' ne."

Hera lit a cigarette. "The rotting man said 'collective.' I wonder what he was talking about." Hera reached into his vest for his tablet and began to scan. "There are three ridite generators running right now in the basement." Hera passed his cigarette to Star so he could finish getting dressed.

Star puffed and released a long drag. "I thought this place was solar powered. You could see them when we walked in?"

"Well, the rotting man is most likely more than just a zombie. It seems this calamlty is a lot more than a preemptive strike."

Hera and Star had their weapons raised in the hallway of the basement. Star was nervous to enter a darkened room. "Ladies first," Hera said, pointing down the hallway.

She smiled a bit and took a step. She turned back to Hera. "Your turn now, Hera," she said with a scared face.

"Star, turn your light to green. Zombies can't see green light and red."

"All right, Hera, I'll take your word for it." Hera and Star quickly turned the corner into a large room.

Hera reached for his tablet in his vest. "There

are at least thirty life signs, but from the readings they are in stasis of some kind."

"Hera, look at that. It looks like a mess of tentacles and computers."

Hera walked up to the mess and touched a keyboard. "Holy hell, I can't read this. It's alien, not English or Kopian. Wait, here's some English."

"What does it say, Hera?"

"We are in a baby-making room for Xenos. Behind this wall is a series of incubation chambers." Hera walked right up to the door and kicked it in. He shined his light to the darkened room. "Pods!"

Hera and Star entered the incubation room and shined their light on three pods. The pods were made of glass and had veins running all over them. "Look at that, Star." The pod occupant was a tall being with gray-brown skin. Veins ran along the chest, which held a head with no eyes.

Star gazed with a puzzled face at the pods. "This one has one long eye running along its head, and the other creature has at least a dozen eyes." Hera and Star jumped at a loud hissing noise coming from around the corner of the incubation room.

"Take the left, Star. I got the right." Hera and star raced over to opposite sides of the row of pods. "What the hell?" Hera said.

Hera's and Star's lights shined on a being standing near an open pod, stretching its arms for the first time. The being looked up at Hera with its many lime-green eyes. "Intruders."

Hera turned his head to Star. "Ah, what was that you said?"

"I said 'intruders.'" The newly born alien reached for the keypad on its pod. Three more pods opened up, giving birth to beings just like him. All three stretched and yawned for their first breath of air. "We have intruders in the incubation room. Kill them before they touch anything."

"Like hell you will," Star said, jumping at it with a knife in hand, only to be swatted and sent flying into the middle of the open room. The three mutated beings boxed Hera. Hera parried every blow with his black sword. All three beings laughed as Hera hacked them away.

Star ran back into the fight, firing her pistol at the one who swatted her. The being fell over its pod, grabbing its chest. Hera and Star walked up to the injured alien. "What are you?" Star asked.

"We have no name. There's no need to introduce ourselves to other life forms we intend on destroying."

Hera bent over the being. "Why did your species cause the calamity and destroy our empire?"

"We hibernated in a Coelum Simia world that was not a part of your empire. They woke us, and we proceeded to annihilate, as we always do. And surprisingly, after a billion years of existence, we met a species with power to destroy us, so we sent the spheres to all your worlds."

"Why are you doing this to us, or anyone for that matter?"

"We destroyed sentient species to replenish our own that are in our path. We are searching."

"Searching? Searching for what?"

"Home." The being's last words were almost sad to Hera's and Star's ears.

Hera reached into his vest and handed Star his tablet. "Go back to the computer and download all that you can squeeze on the tablet."

"Okay, Hera, what about you?"

"I'm going to overload those ridite generators and destroy this place."

1130 Hours

Hera and Star perched themselves on a small store roof. Hera held his tablet in his hand and looked at Star, who was stuffing junk food and cigarettes into her backpack. "How big will the explosion be, Hera?"

"There's only one way to find out, Star," Hera said, smiling at her.

Hera and Star gazed at the pyramid rupture to ash into the lime-green opaque sky. "Cool," Star said. They watched the mushroom grow larger as the shock wave continued in their direction. "Hey, Hera."

"Hold on, Star." The shock wave engulfed the store with fire and ash. Hera and Star hung onto the roof, flapping in the wind like flags.

"Oh, shit, Hera!" Star lost her grip and was taken by the shock wave. Hera let go and flew through ash and scorching wind. Hera caught up with Star midair. He raised his hand into the shock wave, sending a white blast of energy into the radiating wind.

Hera landed on all fours, with Star on his back.

The shock wave died down into an ashen wind. "You okay, Star?"

"I will be when I get another shower. My hair is all burned up."

Hera laughed, raising his hands into the fallout and catching balls of ash like snow. "Well, we just blew up Palis City, so it will be a while before we can shower again."

"Hey, Hera, is that our RV flying toward us right now?"

Hera turned his head to the sky. "What? That is impossible. Mobile homes don't fly, and they aren't very aerodynamic."

Hera and Star jumped out of the direction of the wild mobile home, only to be caught in another reactor explosion. "Fuck you, Hera, and your bad ideas!"

Palis City Ruins, 1152 Hours

Star was washing her hair with water from her canteen. Hera walked up to her and handed her a towel. "Hera, is it safe to be around all this fallout we are exposing ourselves to?"

"Yeah, we are safe. Ridite generators do not emit harmful radiation. Think of it as a sunny day, and you're going to get a light tan." Hera reached for his tablet and turned it on. "I need to get ahold of my father and tell him of what we found here."

"Hera?"

"Dad, there is something I need to tell you about what we found."

"What is it, son? I have time."

"I believe Star and I just saw the faces of who caused the calamity, and let me tell you they are not adorable."

"I know what you are talking about, Hera. Nil' Ka encountered them a few months ago in their own city."

"Really? What are Nil' Ka and you doing about them?"

"As of now, nothing is to be done. We know of no other of these mutant factories you speak of, counting the one I'm guessing you found. Hera, I don't want you to go after these beings until you bring Star home. You got that? I can't let you waste your life, especially since you all are so close to Nil' Ka."

"Then when can I take her home?"

"A lot of people will want revenge, knowing their destroyers are at their gates. And you will be the savior."

"That's a tall order, but I will be more than happy to kick some ass. Hera out."

"Hera," Star said, pointing to a truck driving down the road.

The dirty truck caked in fallout slowly pulled up to Hera and Star. A middle-aged man waved at them and pulled over. "Do y'all want a lift?"

"Sure," Hera answered.

"Are you all heading south?"

"We are just for the night. Our intent was to stay in town, but it turned to ash. Hera handed the man a flyer. "Read it. It's about a new life in T' ne."

"I've heard of the place," said the man. "But no place is safe anymore, kid."

"It's still worth a try, huh?"

Wasteland, 1204 Hours

Hera had trouble smoking, so he tossed his cigarette over the bed of the truck and looked at the ashen landscape. "Now that I think of it, it is quite funny these roads were once farmland, as far as the eye could see. Now mutated plants twist into the air, reaching for prey that might never come and quench parch lips."

"Do you think those aliens are terraforming simian worlds into their own? I mean simians did that."

"No, not all the mutant life is not their intent but is a by product of their reproduction," he said. "They are looking for home. Maybe there is actually a world nearby, where they are from, and like simians they are lost."

"We destroyed our world intentionally. Maybe they sailed too far from home and lost their way."

"Hera, the creature that attacked us in the pyramid—the rotting man. What is it?"

"Yes, Star, unlike a zombie or a mutant, dead or alive, they all can be killed by destroying the brain. Rotting men are much different. They grow by absorbing life, growing taller and stronger, allowing the parasite to grow from maggots to worms. They form clusters in the body. Each cluster controls one side, providing sight, locomotion, defense, etc.

When you fight a rotting man, you are supposed to attack all tentacles or everywhere to damage the creature. One shot to the cerebellum is not sufficient to strike a beast with a thousand minds in one body."

"We will stop at the next burned-out town."

CHAPTER 4

Wasteland, Forty-Two Miles from Nil' Ka City, Canin Village, October 11, 3577, 2035 Hours

Star was leaning against an air conditioner on Canin Mall. She looked up into the evening sky. She loved how the lime-green radiation turned to red at night and shrouded Lulis. A small planet over the Ad' Drin spun slowly in the night sky, its exposed core ruptured by the sphere's arrival from hyperspace.

Landmasses floated as satellites hugged the loosened atmosphere. Star always wondered if people were still alive on the planet. But at night the planet shined orange from fire racing across the planetoid surface, as a result of unstable geology.

Star held a picture of her mother and her, taken days before the calamity. She held it firm over her lighter as it slowly burned in her hands. She couldn't hold back her tears anymore. They poured freely across her face. The picture was dust in her hands now. She slowly raised her hand and tossed the ashes into the evening wind. "Good-bye, Mom."

Canin Village, October 12, 3577, 0741 Hours

Hera had been awake for a good ten minutes now. He had never slept this long before, but he knew he needed the rest. He walked over to wake Star. Star's cheeks were stained from her tears. Hera placed a hand softly on Star's cheek and pulled her in for a kiss. Star didn't react much to his advances. She gave him a soft smile, brushing her messy hair out of her face. "Was that only a kiss, Hera?"

Hera lay by Star. They were both smiling at each other. Silently she raised a hand to his chest and held her hand over his heart. His heartbeat was strong and fast. Hera placed his hands on hers. "I get to be a man today!"

Canin Village, 0923 Hours

Hera and Star were popping heads of zombies on a bridge they were planning on crossing. Hera took aim with his Magnum, allowing powerful bolts to perforate rotting flesh. Star drew them in by running back and forth, letting them chase her, and Hera illuminated the ones foolish enough to give chase.

"Okay, Hera, that's the last of them. Next time you go."

"Oh, are you winded? You were only running back and forth about thirty times."

Star took a long drink from her canteen and

replied, "It is not as easy as it looks, Hera, especially when you get those fast fuckers."

"Well, it's safe for us to cross now. We are only thirty-nine miles from Nil' Ka now."

"I know. I'm so excited. I can't wait for a hot shower in a real house with warm water, shampoo, and towels that you know are at least clean."

"You are one special cookie, Star. When you live out here and T' ne is living out here, you will learn to appreciate what you have."

"I'm sorry, Hera—" Hera stopped Star midsentence by raising his hand. Hera opened a small green bottle and proceeded to consume the clear liquid. "Hera, what are you taking, and why?"

Hera closed the bottle and tossed it to Star. "I just consumed LSD, Rohypnol, MMD, and two antacids to show you how to have fun and appreciate what you have."

"What the fuck, Hera? What were you thinking? This is not the place, and what do I have to appreciate out here?"

"Me, Star. By the way, I'm hearing cupcakes, and I know that's not normal. Bye, Star, come and get me!"

Star watched Hera run into the village, releasing chi attacks on infected beings. "He can't be fucking serious, that son of a bitch."

"Hera, slow down! You're gonna get yourself killed!" Star caught up with Hera, walking on a zombie he had kicked over. "Hera, you need to stop, all right? You're high."

"Nah, dog, anything is possible on LSD. You can't have *no* in your heart."

Star ran up, shooting the dead that surrounded Hera, who failed to take notice. "Well, I do admit that is true, but not in an apocalypse."

"Weeee!" Hera leaped into the air, flying through a window of a two-story building.

"Oh, for the love of science, Hera, this is not funny." Star jumped through the same window and began to look for Hera. She ran for the nearest door and found Hera using the restroom.

"Oh shit, sorry."

"Sorry, had to go potty."

"Really, Hera, just hurry up and go." Star looked away and stood watch at the door, waiting for Hera to finish relieving himself.

"Hey, Star, you see this? That's my friend."

Star turned and saw Hera playing with a skeleton in the restroom bathtub. "Hera, you realize that man has probably been dead for two years."

"That makes a lot of sense. He does have a strange aroma to him."

Hera ran out of the restroom and ran through a wall. Star stared at the hole in the wall and then looked over to a window. "The window would have been my first choice, but whatever fucking works."

Hera raced through the streets, laughing and tripping several mutants as he ran past. Star followed behind, doing her best to keep up with him. "Hera, slow down. I can't kill the infection and follow you!"

"No, dog, I'm looking for a zombie. Jesus, I know he's around here." Hera sliced a zombie in half and began to dance in place.

"He was not a zombie, Jesus, but I'll dance instead."

"You are not a bad dancer, Hera, but don't quit your day job. Hera, are you ready now to calm down and stop running through the streets?"

Hera looked back at Star with a smile. "I want to live in a castle." Hera began to walk slowly in circles, thinking out loud. "I'm pretty sure I heard that somewhere before. I want to live in a castle."

"Hera, can we go inside and just chill? You'll feel a lot better, I promise."

"No."

"Yes, Hera, let's go."

"I should have chosen acid, not LSD. Star, can I tell you something?"

"Sure, Hera, go ahead. We have all the time in the world."

"Okay, but you have to promise not to freak out, okay?"

"Hera, what can possibly freak me out right now?"

"There are dead people behind you."

Star turned around and saw the whole street filled with dead and mutated bodies, staring motionless back at them.

"Oh shit, Hera, run! Get the hell out of here!"

"I told ya not to freak out!"

Hera leaped onto a four-story building and began

to jump from roof to roof. Star reached the top of the building but did not see Hera. *What? I fucking lost him.* She looked at the floor of the roof, seeing cracks. *Well, a big boy like him is bound to leave some damage. That's my best bet.* Star leaped to at least four buildings before losing Hera's tracks. *Dang, are you serious? How could I lose him? Stay calm, and just listen to shit going down.* Star waited for a good minute without hearing anything happening. "No, nothing, Jesus fuck tits."

She walked over to the edge of the building and looked down. "Hera! Oh, no, he fell." Star jumped down and ran to Hera. "Hera, are you all right? Wait a bloody minute. Why are you humping the ground?"

"I'm not humping the ground. My balls are on fire."

"Well, it looks like you are going to town on the ground, and there's no smoke, so your balls are not on fire."

"Yes, they are. Yes, they are."

Star reached for the small bottle of LSD and spun the bottle in her hands. "Well, what doesn't kill you will make you really high." Star consumed the bottle and put it back in her pocket. "Oh, god, this tastes awful. I think I'm going to hurl." Star fell to her hands and knees, gagging for air. She swatted the pavement. Beads of water floated, as gravity no longer applied. She touched one of the droplets of water. The droplet expanded, making a sphere of blue light that began to change color before fading to ash. She stood on her feet and gazed at Hera. Droplets of water burst into ash, shrouding Hera and the village behind him.

Star waded through the ash and light to receive Hera's hand. He began to spin her in circles. The sky was now leaden, making morning look like evening. Star laughed silently, spinning in Hera's arms. She was at peace. She didn't want to leave his arms. She wondered what he saw on his trip. Lulis hovered overhead, shining through the opaque sky of ash and lime-green radiation. She reached her right hand into the sky.

Radiation condensed around her hand, allowing her to move radiation into any position she wanted. Star waved her hand around her head, letting lime-green energy float over her head like a halo.

"Come on, Star, let's enjoy this high before it fades."

Hera and Star ran through the ash, kicking up clouds of dust, laughing as the planet slowly died around them. Hera waved his hands, clearing the road of ash for them to sit. Star lay on the hot pavement, clearing her face of ash.

Hera danced around her, swinging his arms in the air. Blue strings of light flowed freely from his hands. The energy slowly rained down, turning red and then white before hitting the Ad' Drin. Hera hit the ground, sending the ash around them flying in the air. Ash fell back to the Ad' Drin as flower petals. Star tried to imagine how they would smell if they were real.

She slowly rose to her feet and danced with Hera, kicking up ash and creating more flower petals. Buildings began collapsing to their foundations, with mutated plants growing in their stead. Pillars of tentacles shot dozens of feet into the air, screaming in pain at their sudden birth.

"Get down, Star." Hera slammed Star on the ashen pavement as two long lime-green bolts of plasma collided with Ad' Drin. Pillars of sparks and ash elevated ten feet in the sky. Star slowly turned her head to a growling being on one of the mutated trees. The being looked like the one in Palis City, but larger. The being's head was covered in glowing lime-green eyes with a mask covering its front eyes. Six long pylons grew from its back. The crystal was opaque and black, with parasites swimming around white lights in the pylons.

The being teleported in front of them, roaring before swatting Hera off Star. The being grabbed Star with its long arm. Star kicked and screamed as the being held her in the air with one arm. She turned her head to the being as it finally spoke to her. "I prefer my victims to remain silent at all times."

Bursts of light and sparks erupted from the being's back. It yelled in pain, throwing Star to the ashen floor. The being returned fire, sending long bursts of plasma toward its attackers. More flashes erupted from its body, but it continued to return fire.

Large orange bursts of plasma perforated the long black pylons on the being's back. Hera hastily advanced, firing on the strange being. The creature dropped its weapon, looking up at Hera. "I will not give you the satisfaction of destroying me." Pylons on the being's back pulsated with white light. Hera ran through his body onto Star, who was only feet away.

Star's eyes were still looking up at the being before it transformed into a shock wave of white light. All she remembered was her screaming.

Hotel City, October 13, 3577, 0812 Hours

"Get your hands away from my no-no square."

Hera woke up in a bed, jumping around. Nurses held him down the best they could. "Calm down, please. We don't want to sedate you again."

"Hmm, do you have LSD?"

"No, sir, I believe I don't carry that in stock."

Hera looked at the woman with a frustrated face. "I don't like you."

"Do you really want to do that again, kid—get high in a wasteland and get attacked by god knows what?"

A large man with tan skin entered the room, wearing black fatigues. He walked to Hera's bed and extended his hand to Hera. "Michael Howard."

Hera received his handshake and replied, "Hera Kila' Ka. I presume you are the leader here?"

"Yes, I am. Hera, are you feeling all right to take a walk?"

"Yes, sir, I am."

"Good, wake your friend and meet me outside in a few."

Hera and Star buckled from the light of the planet's sun and stumbled to lean against the makeshift hospital. "So, Howard, what is your situation here, and where are we? I know we are not in Space Alaska."

"Walk with me. I'll explain. We have the hangar on the right, but no aircraft. The fence line extends around the villas, then into the valley in front of us. The schools are to the center, and most of us live in the main hotels."

"How many people live here in this village of yours, Howard?" Hera asked.

"Three hundred souls. Most are kids with no family. Some are family units or friends. We came together before finding this place. Guards are posted 24/7, and newcomers are quarantined for three days. Stuff like that."

"Wait, Star and I were only quarantined for one day. What's up with that?"

"You all were crashing from y'alls LSD trip. When you two were examined, we noticed your old bite marks. You two are immune."

Star walked over to a tree and lay down against the trunk. "I am going to burn one right here."

Hera and Howard walked over and joined Star for a smoke. "Howard, that being that attacked Star and me—have you encountered them before?"

"Yes, Hera, we call that one Warper, since it possesses the ability to teleport and is a simian-size foot soldier."

"They are the faces of the calamity. They destroyed our world and countless simians' worlds with one blow."

"Who are they, Hera?"

"I don't know. The being Star and I encountered in Palis City didn't say they had a name. All they want is to look for their home."

"They burned the stars, looking for a place that might not exist."

"Howard, how are you on supplies in your village?"

"We get everything from Canin Village, but the place is almost picked clean now from us and others passing by town."

Hera stood on his feet with a smile. "Howard, I believe I can help you with that."

Hotel City, Billeting Office, 0901 Hours

Hera, Star, and Howard sat in the break room in the billeting office. Hera leaned his tablet against a pile of discarded boxes. "I'm going to get in touch with my father in T' ne. He will be able to help you here, Howard." The screen displayed an image of a phone that rang a few times before Hera's dad appeared on-screen. "Dad, you told me about a year ago you were looking for a place for an outpost for T' ne and Nil' Ka. I believe I found a place for you all."

"Yes, Hera, we are looking for one, but none are secure for long-term operations."

"Dad, I found a place that might work, if the leader agrees."

Howard leaned forward in view of the tablet. "Hello there, I am Michael Howard."

"Hello, Victor Kila' Ka. Mr. Howard, what are you looking for in this treaty?"

"Supplies, manpower, and foremost the right to be independent from other countries, like you."

"You and your town will remain independent. T' ne will follow your laws and protocols. As long as we are stationed in your village, supplies will pour in. We promise security and the ability for you to maintain your village."

Howard looked away for a moment, quickly deciding. "That's the best news I've heard in two years. I agree to the terms."

"All right, then watch the skies. Supplies are on their way."

Howard stood up and shook Hera's and Star's hands. "Thank you both; your supplies will help my people greatly."

"Let's go wait for the supplies my father is sending. I am kind of surprised to see what he is sending you."

They all ran out of the billeting office. Star pointed to the sky as ten drones passed over the mountains into the middle of the village. "That was quick, Hera."

"We are a lot closer to the coast now. T' ne and Nil' Ka are closer than ever."

Howard yelled to three people standing near a truck. "Hey, you three, help receive the supplies coming."

The drones hovered overhead, slowly lowering their payload to the Ad' Drin. Most of the boxes were small, but all were labeled with a packing roster. Howard began to laugh out loud. "Weapons and ammo. Your father sent us weapons and ammo."

Hera jumped over the piles of supplies to Howard. "What weapons? I want to see what he sent."

A tall woman walked over to the supplies and opened a crate that read "Fruits." She plucked a grape from its vine and smiled.

"Kimberly Amaya, is that you?" Hera said, walking over to the tall girl eating grapes.

"Hera, oh my god! I haven't seen you since AIT. I knew you would survive all of this."

Hera gave her a big hug and introduced her to Star. "Star, this is Kimberly Amaya. We went to school and AIT together."

"Hi there," Star said, reaching for a handshake from Kimberly.

"You all are traveling together, or did you just meet?"

"We just met, and we are traveling together. I am escorting her to T' ne."

"Oh, Hera helping people—that's a first. I've heard stories of a boy who tells people where to go for safety. But that's all he does. He claims he doesn't want the responsibility of moving people through the mutated wastelands."

"I had an extreme change of heart, and I want a break from running day by day. I'll return home with Star only for a short time. Then I'm coming back out."

Howard walked up to the three. "They are going to organize the supplies. I've got to get back to my class."

"You are a teacher, Howard?" Star asked.

"Yes, I am. After I got out of the army, I decided teaching was the best for me. All my family members were teachers. Do y'all want to come to my class?"

1024 Hours

"All right, kids, pull out your journals, and let's write a quick story on your experience in the waste."

Howard started to pull out bags from a locker behind his desk as kids wrote in their journals. "Hey, Kimberly, are these kids orphans, or do they still have family?" Star asked.

"Yes, most of these kids are orphans. Three months ago three busloads of kids and teenagers came through our gate. The teenagers make most of our workforce, but they protected the younger kids for one and a half years before they came here. The younger kids still go to school, run by the adults, and the teenagers work and provide security."

"So what exactly do you do here, Kimberly?"

"Whatever the fuck I want."

Hera and Star burst out with laughter. Hera stood up and turned to the two and stretched. "All this learning is making me tired. Come on, let's go burn one."

"So how did you come upon this place, Kimberly? I figure you are like me and forever roam the wastelands."

"No, that was my intent, but after a fight a few

months ago, I encountered those strange beings, so I came here. More people, more protection."

"So you have encountered them before. I guess there are a lot more of those beings out here."

"Yes, Hera. What are you going to do, Hera— start a one-man war on alien invaders? People have enough just waking up in the morning."

Hera looked at the scattered Lulis hanging overhead and then turned back to Kimberly. "If we stand behind our walls and let them grow in numbers, there will be no more morning skies for us. We all will be part of their collective for sentient less beings with no true purpose. I will tell you this. I don't want my loved ones to suffer another calamity."

Hera flicked his cigarette onto the road. "When Star is safe in T' ne, I will make it my personal goal to find them where they're hiding and bring death to them all."

Hera was trampled by a wave of students running with guns in their hands. Star extended a hand to Hera. "Where are they going packing heat?"

"My class is going to shoot some zombies that hang around the fence."

"Howard, is that safe? They are just kids, after all."

"Yes, it is, Hera. We are in a new world. Everyone needs to learn how to defend themselves. Would you have these kids cowering in the corner or fighting for their own lives?"

"I guess you're right. Best for them to learn not

to be afraid of the monsters. It would be awesome to have generations ready to survive this world."

"They are the future, Hera. Come on, it's going to be fun."

Kids took turns shooting mutants and undead, clinging to the compound fence. Random shots were fired all over. Hera walked over to the kids and decided to give them some advice. "You can kill the infected by shooting them in their bodies, but what you want is head shots."

Hera quickly drew his Magnum. It spun in his hand, whining to life. Kids jumped as a large bolt of plasma vaporized the infected along the compound fence. "You see, extremely fucking affective."

A young man approached Howard and began to speak. "Excuse me, sir, I don't mean to interrupt your class, but we got a large crate with meat and we have no working freezers."

"Oh, don't worry about that," Hera said, spinning his weapon in his hand and almost dropping it. "If there's one thing I can do, that's fix refrigerators. Always had a knack for fixing stuff and blowing things up."

"Thank you, Hera. Once the freezers are fixed, we will have a barbecue for you all."

"Okay, then I'm off to work. See ya at dinnertime, bitches."

Hotel City, Under the Stars, 1958 Hours

Everyone in the village stuffed themselves with meat and fresh fruits. Teenagers danced around the bonfire, swinging their arms and howling at the night. Howard played an electric guitar while Kimberly beat on drums. Howard stopped the music, yelling for a story to be told. Kids yelled for Hera to tell a story.

Kimberly yelled for Hera. "Hey, Hera, tell us a story from your adventures in the wastelands."

"Okay, I will tell a story but not of my adventures. It's a story of a species who wants the universe only to find someone more powerful and a billion years ahead. In the year 2327—or 45,943 in dog years—a young species was on the verge of launching their first generation ship into deep space. They knew not of alien life. It was still a mystery. One year before the ship completion, an alien species came into their own solar system.

"This new species terraform a small red planet in as little as a year before making contact with the young species. They promised the wonders of the known galaxy. Contact was made, and friendship was quickly sewn tight. But the young species was jealous. They wanted to terraform the solar system's fourth planet. They wanted to discover new species and forge an empire.

"Not to be annexed into an existing empire, they sank back into their home world and finished their generation ship. The engine roared to life. They aimed for the fourth planet. The young species made planets fall, jumping out of their generation ship. Soaring through the planet's thin atmosphere, the species' near-suicidal planet descent vaporized newly established cities.

"When the dust cleared, billions of the young

species raced across the red planet on all fours. The tall, frail humanoids were ripped apart by the millions. All that the newcomers achieved on the small red planet was devoured in only one night.

"With newly acquired technology, new ships had been built in as little as a decade. Billions waited to conquer the stars and devour worlds, just like what happened on the fourth planet. Before they left, they turned their weapons to their home world and fired on tectonic plates.

"The blue world became geologically unstable. Quakes ripped mountains to rubble, tidal waves salted fertile valleys, and fire raced across lush forest. Their home secure from anyone—alien or colonist—they turned their massive terraforming fleets to the heavens.

"Countless alien species were found to populate the galaxy. In every world they visited, they told the natives they wanted to be friends, which was true to an extent. The upper atmosphere of worlds was blackening, with the promise that we wanted to be friends, but to be friends we must first kick your ass.

"If you put up a fight, only then can we be friends, and if deemed weak, every single world your species crawls and hides will be destroyed. All bio matter devoured every last puddle drank. Your planet mined to a barren husk, spinning in darkness.

"The young species kept true to their promise, giving life to the strong species and giving death to the weak species. When they exhausted their resources, they returned to their home world to build a capital, but upon their return all remaining in the system were gone.

"They left in arks, massive ships carrying the remainder of their population. These ships traveled farther into the galaxy and even left the home galaxy for neighboring galaxies. The young species was content in their work and retreated to their new homes, leaving the home system as a sanctuary.

"The species' empire flourished for more than a thousand years, with no contest by conquered species. Not until one summer morning did four spheres change everything. People could feel the spheres approach through hyperspace hours before they arrived. The spheres pierced the morning skies, exploding into waves of lime-green energy that blanketed the stars day and night. Well, there's no need to finish the rest. I'm pretty sure y'all can figure the rest out."

Kimberly stood up and threw a piece of fruit at Hera. "Wow, Hera, way to be a fucking buzzkill. I'm going to bed."

"What? My father used to tell that story. I thought it was a lovely story."

"Not for kids, Hera. They have enough on their hands. They don't need to start thinking the calamity is punishment for past transgressions."

"Hera, there's something I need to ask you, if you are interested."

"Sure, Howard, feel free to ask me anything."

"Those beings that attacked you during your LSD trip, they are nearby, some of them."

"Where are they located, Howard?"

"Just outside of town in an old warehouse. It will be heavily guarded with the undead, but I'm sure we can destroy them."

"Do you have a plan, or do you want to go in guns a blazing?"

"I do have a plan, Hera, and it's quite simple. I and my crew make a diversion, and you and Star blow it up from the inside."

"I'm not going to lie, Howard. That sounds like a terrible plan, but I'm sure we can make it work."

"Good. Take a nap. We leave at 0300 hours."

CHAPTER 5

Canin Village, October 14, 3577, 0324 Hours

Hera, Star, Kimberly, and Howard ran into position, along with about twenty men. Howard handed Hera binoculars. Hera scanned the old building. Large pylons rose into the canopy. A large parasite swam around lime-green lights. One Warper stood outside with at least a dozen smaller versions.

Hera pondered why some zombies and mutants had green pylons sticking out from their backs and some didn't. He turned and handed the binoculars to Star.

"So how are you planning on distracting these guys?"

Kimberly loaded a missile into the under sling missile launcher of her weapon. "See those glowing pylons? They explode if you do a lot of damage," Kimberly said, pointing at the pylons.

"And I will fight the Warper," Howard said, "since I know blink, short-range teleportation."

"I will be able to sense where it goes easier and

most likely survive a fight against one Hera," Said Howard.

"Star, in case one of us gets there first, here's my second tablet." Star took the tablet and put it in her vest. "The tablet is already set up for overloading any reactors. Just hook it up and turn the device on."

"All right, Kimberly, ready?" Hera hadn't finished his sentence before Kimberly detonated one of the pylons.

Hera and Star charged to the burning hole of the warehouse. Most of the pylon and no pylon mutants were dispatched from the explosion. Hera and Star made it into the warehouse with no resistance. Hera spun in a 360-degree clearing to every corner of the building.

"Star, overload the reactors in the back—just one. Don't worry about all of them. I'll stand guard."

"Shit, I really hope Howard was able to catch the Warper." Hera heard a thud and saw a figure fall from the ceiling. The figure slowly rose, wearing nothing but tattered pants. It had long arms connected to a skinny frame, and it roared at Hera.

Hera parried multiple lime-green bursts from the small being's weapon, sending them flying back on the creature. Hera jumped into the air, allowing his blade to fall on the being's head. He kicked his blade free from the being.

He brought his sword to his face and smelled

the black viscous liquid clinging to the edge of the blade.

"Hmm, smells like burned cookies. How are we going back there, Star? Do you need an adult?"

"I just need twenty more seconds for the program to install."

"Okay, let me give you a hand." Hera ran for Star. He was only ten yards away when another figure appeared in view.

The Warper was covered in black blood from head to toe. It grabbed Hera and tried to pin Hera to the floor. "We must construct additional pylons. We must construct!" Hera broke free from the Warper's clutch, spinning around to the being's back. Hera ripped one of the creature's pylons and then stabbed the pylon into a cluster of smaller pylons in its upper back.

"Fuck your pylons," Hera said, kicking the Warper through the warehouse walls. "Okay, now that he's taken care of …"

Star handed Hera the tablet. "I couldn't understand the alien interface. I can't switch it to English like you did."

"Just press down to the end of the page, and click the last word," Hera said, performing the action.

"There, English. Yes, I want to initiate the overload of ridite reactors."

"What's taking so long, Hera?"

"It's downloading the file right now," Hera said, looking at the terminal screen.

"And you said plug and play."

"Hey, how was I to know an aliens computers run off a different operating system?"

"Ah, here we are. Wait, no, I don't want to download PC Optimizer, Great Deals Toolbar. Fuck."

Hera slowly turned his head to Star. "What now?"

"The file is processing now. Ten more minutes."

Star looked at the hole in the warehouse. Plasma bolts flowed back and forth. She turned her head back to Hera, who had a guilty smile.

"Fuck it." Star walked over to the generators and began to fire at the tops of all the generators. Sparks flew from each one. Hera looked at his tablet and proceeded to scream. "What!" Hera ran for the exit, screaming and waving his arms.

Star paused for a second and noticed all the beings had stopped firing and were staring at Hera. They were just amazed to see a grown man screaming like a child, running away from the battle.

"Why are you screaming, Hera?" Kimberly asked.

Hera ran past Kimberly and Howard and continued screaming into the forest. Hera comically jumped over a fallen tree while screaming at the top of his lungs.

"Why is he screaming, Star?" Howard asked.

"His program was taking too long, so I shot the generators. Then he started to scream like a pussy."

"Well, I would scream too if you shot at a reactor."

"Oh, okay then," Star replied.

Everyone hit the Ad' Drin as the warehouses front exploded, blanketing the beings in fire. Hera slowly raised his head over the log and looked over the burning building.

"Ha! The explosion wasn't that big, and here I was screaming like a little bi—" Another explosion ripped into the forest, sending everyone off their feet. Hera climbed over several fallen trees, leaned over, and saw much of the building was still intact. "Star, get up. We need to see if the building is cleared."

Hera and Star ran to the burning building. All the beings were dead. Hera climbed the smoldering rubble.

"What are you looking for, Hera? This place is ruined," Kimberly said.

"There's something here. I can hear it calling for help."

"She's right, Hera. All the mutants are dead. This place is a wreck. Let's go. We need to leave before there is another explosion," Star said.

"Y'all can't hear it. It's calling out for help. The voice is getting fainter. Help me."

Hera and Kimberly lifted a large piece of wreckage. Hera jumped in a pit of rubble and began to dig.

"What is he looking for?"

"He says he hears something calling for help. I

don't hear anything," Star said, answering Howard's question.

Hera emerged from the pit, carrying a large mutant insect. The insect resembled a large fly. Hera laid the large insect on the ground and began to remove debris from the injured being.

"Hera, what is that?"

"I don't know, Star. This is the first time I've seen an insect as a mutant before."

The mutant extended one of its arms to Hera. Hera slowly received the mutant's invitation. He looked up to find the mutant gone, along with everyone else. Hera slowly rose to take in his new decor. Mountains hung in the night sky, with giant tentacles rising toward the lime-green light. One singularity lit the planet in a lime-green haze but was outshined by a large barred spiral galaxy overhead. Hera looked back down. The mutant fly rose into the air and spoke. "This is our home world. This is what we dream every night, Hera."

"Who the hell are you all?"

"We have no name. Our only purpose is to make it here."

Hera blinked and looked around. He was back in reality. He looked back down at the mutant.

"It is dead, Hera," Star said, placing a hand on his shoulder. "Come on, we need to get out of here."

"Howard, Star and I will take our leave from here. I hope we meet again someday and do many drugs."

"Hera, why are you leaving so soon? Did that creature tell you something?"

"Yes, Kimberly, it did. Their home world—I need to get to T' ne as quickly as I can."

Howard extended his hand to Hera. "Well, Hera, I hope we do meet again. Take Star to T' ne."

"All right, kept me posted on what goes on out here, Howard," Hera said, receiving Howard's hand.

"Let's move, Star. We are only forty miles from Nil' Ka. We can make it by tomorrow."

Howard and Kimberly watched Hera and Star disappear into the forest. "He's the boy who will save us all."

"Do you really think so, Howard?"

"Yes, he was born for this, nothing else. You know a hero when you meet one—and a killer. Hera's all of them rolled into one."

Wasteland, Twenty-Eight Miles from Nil' Ka City, October 14, 3577, 1021 Hours

Hera and Star plowed their way through the mutated forest. Each footstep woke the roots of the trees above them. Limbs reached for Hera and Star. Small tentacles whipped the air, releasing spines that gave chase into the air.

Hera leaped through an opening, spinning his sword, blocking the last spines sent by the mutant trees. "There, that open field," Hera said.

Hera and Star leaped one more time into the air through the mutant canopy. They landed on an unused plot of land. Hera walked over to a pile of hay bales and rested. "Okay, red apples under a mutant tree are testicles, not apples."

"Who would have guessed trees had balls, Hera?"

"Who would have guessed trees could yell at the top of their leaves? Not this guy."

"Hera, what are those things?"

Hera ducked Star behind the hay bales. "I don't know, Star."

"Look, there's one dead near the exit of the barn. Stay low."

Star laughed at Hera, who tried to move tactically but tripped into a hole covered by tall grass.

Hera slowly rose above the grass, holding a pair of binoculars to his face. "No amount of awesomeness will redeem you for past incidents, Hera."

"One can only try, Star."

"Is the coast clear, Hera?"

"Seems to be. We need to check out the barn. Those floating creatures must have come out of it."

Hera jumped out of the hole and raced to the barn door. Star caught up to him and waited for his signal. Hera nodded his head and charged into the barn. "Clear."

"Same here, Hera."

Hera walked up to a few bodies of cattle. "They must have come out of their bodies just recently. They don't stink yet." Hera walked up to the dead mutant at the barn entrance. He reached for his tablet to scan the body. "This can't be right. I'm getting mixed radiation—several, to be exact."

"What are you getting, Hera?"

"Well, I'm getting the radiation in the sky, just more concentrated, and if I am reading this right, neutrinos."

"Neutrinos!"

"This creature has an FTL drive. From my reading, this creature is a baby ship."

Hera waved his tablet back and forth on the mutant. He handed Star the tablet for her opinion.

"Rooms. This little ship has rooms already growing inside it. Are you serious? But why grow it out here? I would want to grow it at my mutant factory."

"No, It must be part of the natural evolution of the aliens. Mutant plus mutant equals rotting man."

"Rotting man makes base and soldiers from mutants running about."

"And these grow naturally like the rotting man," Star added. "Hera, how far are we from Nil' Ka City?"

"We are twenty-eight miles out, but let's take a rest. It's about to rain, and I haven't had breakfast."

Wasteland, 1201 Hours

"That creature said we can't stop them. It said we will find home."

"What, Hera?"

"That mutant fly creature showed me an image of its home planet. It was beautiful—tall mountains, skies as lime green as our skies, and quiet. From the way he spoke to me, they must have traveled a long way to get to our galaxy."

"So you don't think they are from our neighborhood, Hera? You think they are from a distant part in the universe." Star shook her head from side to side. "That doesn't make sense, Hera. Why go through all this trouble to find it? They have to know it is their home world. And they have to know where it is."

"Something must have happened to them. Why did they come from another part of the universe, and why can't they find their home?" Hera took a long drink from his canteen. "They are just kids who are orphaned by space. Their home world might not even exist. It could just be an idea they all share. They must be looking for a way out of life."

"You're saying they are trying to ascend, Hera?"

"Yes, Star, I am, and if this home world actually exists and if just one touches ground—"

"There goes the universe," Star said, interrupting Hera. "My mother, Hera, always told me we believe in god not because he created the universe, but because others want to be like him. And to be like him is wrong. We are not fit to be gods. We are only fit to lie beneath him."

"And where is your mother now, Star?"

"Dead. Running about in the waste. Zombiefied,"

Star said roughly. "Bio matter for the masses of mutant warriors."

"Damn, girl, hate her much?"

Star laughed to herself. "No, no, she was a fool, and that got her killed. No more talking. Let's get back to running the ultrathon to Nil' Ka."

Hera stood and looked at Star with a smile. "Ready, set, and go."

Both of them took off. Hera tripped, and Star tripped over him. Star popped her head over the grass. "Do ya think you can use your tablet to scan for holes in the ground, Hera?"

Wasteland, 1854 Hours

"We are making good timing, faster than I thought."

"Yeah, if it wasn't for all this fucking rain, we might be there today."

"Maybe there's a reason behind all this rain," Star suggested.

"What, Star, divine intervention?"

"I don't know, maybe. Anything's possible, Hera."

"I don't believe that, Star. You're talking about predestined destiny, and that means no free will—none whatsoever."

"If you believe you have free will, but believe someone has a plan for you in the end, even if you change your mind at the last second, and go the other way—that is not free will."

"Someone knows the outcome, and every

decision you make only to have you die three days from now means predestined destiny."

"I don't believe that, Hera. I wouldn't be standing here if I did. Hell, I wouldn't be alive if I had stayed back in the church with my mother. Hera, how far are we from Nil' Ka now?"

"I say fifteen miles maybe. You're thinking about running into the night, huh?"

"Yes, I want to get there as quickly as possible, Hera. I want to go home now."

"Well then, Star, let's run regardless of the weather, situation, and encounters of the lime-green sky."

Hera gave his hand to Star with a soft smile. "Ready, Star?"

"Yes."

Nil' Ka City, October 14, 3577, 2303 Hours

"Come on, Star, the gates are right there. We made it, babe." Star's face was white against the red night. "I want a shower, damn it."

"Well, let's go just one more hundred-yard sprint and we are at the gates. Push it out."

Hera and Star raced on all fours, Ad' Drin ripping under determined paws. Hera leaped into the air, spinning with no control until he came crashing down at a guard's feet. The young guard handed Hera a water bottle. "Take me to your leader." Star came crashing into a truck, knocking it off its wheels. "And infirmary for her."

Hera and Star were led by two guards into a large room under the city. A middle-aged man was waiting for them. "Have a seat, Hera, as well as your friend."

"Sami Hedrick, we meet at last."

"Hi, I'm Star Cassidy, Hera's friend and the reason we are here."

"Here, Hera, your father has not told ya the situation the city is in, has he?"

"No, he has not, but from what I heard from him the last time he spoke to you, he said, 'Suck twenty dicks and die.'"

"Our city will be soon under siege, Hera."

"Under siege? Under siege from whom?"

"Kopian defected from the city a couple months back. They up and left thousands of them and met up with thousands more. They declared themselves free from simian control and furthermore took up residence in a base where we were getting supplies."

"What do they have that you so desperately need? Your city looks so well-off."

"Two weapons. They can destroy the city, and they declared this the first since the majority of them came from here."

"And they attack tomorrow at noon."

"Well, have y'all sat down and talked with them? Shit, I mean, what is all this aggression coming from?"

"I don't know, Hera. Where are the hostilities coming from? All we got was a radio call saying our destruction and the name of their new country."

"But their Kopi, sir, a simian child, is three times

stronger than the lot of them. Even a Kopi soldier is weaker than simians."

"Star, that would be their downfall, but with those two weapons, they are unstoppable."

"Sami, what do the weapons do exactly?" Hera asked.

The weapon is one large mobile missile array. One single shot becomes ten, each choosing to attack land or air targets of their own will."

"But with you and Star, we might have a chance."

"Sorry, I don't believe in chance, just random happenstance."

"When my soldiers are feeding on Kopian soldiers and they're too busy fighting for their lives, you two can slip in and disable the weapon. I, of course, will send other teams in if you all fail to achieve the objective."

"Sounds like a terrible plan, but if we do this for you, we want a ride to T' ne by land or preferably air."

"I'll see what I can do, Hera. My pilots are skittish about flying with that weapon far from the city walls, especially with the platforms lobbing shells."

Hera extended his hand to Sami in agreement. Sami took Hera's hand. "This will be your room. I will have food and beds sent to you."

"Thank you, Sami."

"Guards, give these folks anything they want. They have a hell of a day ahead of them."

Nil' Ka City, October 15, 3577, 0803 Hours

Star was finishing lacing up her boots when Hera walked in. He was wearing a black leather jacket, shredded camouflage pants, and a matching sash hanging off his waist. Hera raised gold bug shield to his eyes. "What I dress according to the apocalypse at hand."

"You have been through other apocalypses, Hera?"

"No, I have not, but if I'm going to kick ass, I'm dressing."

"Gay!"

"No, Star, I dress—"

Hera was interrupted by a young woman who entered their room. "Lieutenant Ybarra, I will be y'alls pilot. If y'all are ready, follow me."

Hera and Star jumped in the bed of the gator as the lieutenant headed for the airfield. "Here, that disk contains the program to shut the weapons down."

"There will be a terminal on the right of each platform. I'm sure you can figure the rest out."

"How far will you take us?"

"We are not getting within one mile of the weapon, in fear it will be our last flight. Everyone will have to head over on foot. We will still provide air support. That's all."

"Fine by me. Looks like we are here."

Hera and Star jumped off and headed for Sami, already boarding an aircraft.

"Hera, we're counting on you and Star. Race through and kill only what are in your path, for every second the weapons are online, more beings will die."

"No problem. I love killing as much as I love saving them, and that's third on my list."

"So what is second on your list, Hera?"

"Cinnamon raisin bagels," Hera said with a smile. "May our fathers help us?"

Lieutenant Ybarra motioned Hera and Star to her drop ship. "Jump on. Get in the Gunner Spot Star. Hera, you can be my copilot."

"Do not you have one, Ybarra?"

"I worked at a beauty salon before the calamity, Hera. It was fly or become a mutant. I chose fly, and that got me here."

"AL righty, ready when you are."

Lieutenant Ybarra typed a passcode into the small screen in the instrument panel. "All right, APU on. Don't have time to preflight all the rest of the shit. Moving PCLs forward, and those loud bangs are the plasma spheres igniting." Ybarra stared at the screen in the instrument panel. "Three, two, one, okay, we're off."

The drop ship quickly lifted into the air. Star could see at least a dozen fighters, follow as well. She never had seen a view of the planet from the sky. The horizon hazed lime green, and smog formed burning cities. Star stuck her head out of the gunner window to get a better look. She could see Kopian forces en masse around the weapons array, as well as enemy fighters circling in formation.

"One minute out. Everyone, get ready to jump

out. Hera, get armed. Grab the copilot's cyclic stick and return fire. Soften the crowd before I drop you all off."

Hera squeezed the trigger, sending four long streams of weapon fire into the Kopi formation. He quickly lifted his aim to a Kopian fighter racing toward them. Hera yelled over the ICS to Star, "Killing is my favorite thing, Star." Hera was firing randomly into the crowd. "I think this is as far as we are going to get. Star, jump out." Hera leaped from the copilot's seat, falling forty meters to the Ad' Drin under them. He looked back up into the sky. Nil' Kan soldiers leaped from their drop ships. Hera looked to his right. Star was by his side.

Others lined up on the line, yelling at the top of their lungs, blowing horns into the air. Hera and Star houled in beat with everyone else. "This is pretty fun, Hera," Star said to him. "Men and women get to play again. Oh shit, game on."

Hera and Star raced on all fours, with everyone else jumping out of the way of enemy fire. Hera leaped into the air, four limbs out in front of him like a monkey jumping tree to tree. His body came crashing down, leaving a Kopi soldier's body in ruins. He quickly grabbed another, throwing it to the ground, releasing its head from its shoulders.

Star landed in front of two Kopi soldiers, grabbing them by their weapons. She easily tossed their frail bodies into the air. She swiftly delivered another blow to a Kopi, raising her weapon to her. Star watched as the Kopian soldier was sent flipping into the air comically. "I'm gonna have too much fun with this."

Hera swung his sword with deadly aim, slicing Kopian bodies without much effort. He raised his Magnum, firing into a squad of enemy soldiers. Bright-orange bolts perforate bodies in bright-yellow clouds of fire and smoke.

Hera suddenly hit the floor, dodging a long red bolt. He slowly rose to his feet with a smile. "Finally, a challenge at hand." An actual Kopian soldier stood in his path. It had dark-red skin to match its red armor. It stood a foot taller than its gray-skin counterparts.

The Kopian soldier aimed his staff weapon at Hera, inviting him to fight. He jumped into the air and came crashing down on the staff weapon. The ground under the soldier's feet scattered under Hera's attack. He swung his weapon, parrying Hera's relentless attacks. What the Kopi lacked in strength he made up in skill.

Hera grunted as every attempt to damage his opponent was thwarted. He fell to the ground as the staff weapon slapped his face. Hera dropped his sword and grabbed onto his assailant's weapon. Hera lifted the Kopian soldier into the air and then slammed him into the Ad' Drin. Hera jumped on top of the soldier and, in a fit of rage, began to beat the Kopi to death.

Orange blood poured out of the Kopi's mouth and nose. Hera reached for the Kopi's face. He ripped the top part of its head off. He roared in victory. He kicked the head into the crowd. "I'm so high." Hera leaped back into the air in a backflip and landed on the weapons array platform. He swatted Kopi soldiers out of his way until he got to one of the terminals.

Hera inserted the disk and waited for it to power down the weapon. He then returned fire in battle. "Where the hell is Star?" Hera ducked as a large explosion ripped the air in front of him. He heard laughing above and saw Star flipping in the air out of control.

Star landed on top of the other weapon and grabbed hold of one of the large servos. She tugged until hydraulic fluid sprayed into the air. She then did a stage dive into a group of Kopi trying to advance on the weapons array. "I need to ask her to be my Facebook friend." Hera looked back into the battle. Kopi began to lower their weapons in defeat. "That was quick. I mean, it's only been maybe twenty minutes. Kopian are no fun," Hera yelled.

He jumped down to Star and gave her a hand. She was covered in Kopian blood and hydraulic oil from head to toe. "Did you get pictures?"

Star laughed and responded to Hera, "No, I unfortunately couldn't find the gift shop."

Hera looked back down to the ground and found Lieutenant Ybarra feeding on a Kopi corpse. "Lieutenant Ybarra, what the hell are you doing down here?"

She raised her head and swallowed a mouthful of her meal. "I got shot down, came crashing out of the sky like a ton of cement feathers."

Hera and Star looked in front of them and saw Ybarra's mangled drop ship. "That might explain the large explosion."

"Well, how did she survive?"

"Shhh." Hera stopped Star and motioned her away. "I'm sure that's of no importance. Let her finish her lunch."

Hera and Star jumped onto the LMTV. Hera reached for a cigarette from his pocket and slowly lit it. He passed the smoke to Star. Hera threw his feet onto the corpse of Kopi soldiers that filled the bed of the truck. He covered the bodies with the truck's tarp and looked at Star. "Looks like Turkey casserole tonight."

Nil' Ka City, October 15, 3577, 1452 Hours

Hera and Star were waiting on the airfield for Sami. He slowly approached, carrying a large tablet under his right arm. "As I promised, if you help me, I can help you."

"I get it if you can't have the weapon. No one can. That sounds about right, huh?"

"Hera, you two saved thousands of lives today."

"And we destroyed a thousand more, but who cares, eh?"

"The fighter you're sitting on is your ride home. Hera, get in. Start it. Fly away."

"All right then, Star, hop in the back." Hera put on the pilot's headset and turned back to Sami.

"I hope this means our two countries are allies again?"

"Always, Hera."

Hera closed the cockpit canopy as Star keyed over the ICS. "Hey, Hera, I'm assuming since you jumped in the pilot seat, you know how to fly one of these things, huh?"

"I was a part of a visionary unit, Star. We maintained and operated our own equipment, as well as fought three MOSs in one. Well, that's what I was trained for. Then the apocalypse happened. Never really battle tested."

"Oh, okay, then I better buckle up then." Hera pulled on the collective stick, raising the fighter in the air. "Take a nap, Star. We are almost home. We are almost home."

CHAPTER 6

Wasteland, Twenty Miles from Nil' Ka City, October 14, 3577, 1125 Hours

"Bird, bird, birdie. Look, dog, dog, little puppy." Hera and Star were taking a break, naming items that passed their way. "So, Hera, is this what television is at the end of the world?"

"I wouldn't call it passing time. I would call it a hobby."

Star bent her arm and grabbed Hera's hand. "What happens once we get to T' ne, Hera?"

"I don't know, most likely go our separate ways. You know I am a whore. I might start up a gentlemen's club or two."

"Oh, okay. That's cool, I guess." Star slowly let go of Hera's hand, but he quickly went back and grabbed hold of hers.

"Star, you know I'm messing with ya, right? I didn't mean to fall in love with you. In fact, I thought I would die out here. But apparently I'm too good in the business of killing mutants. And if it is going to be bitches for days, I want to wake up in a pile of half-dead bitches with you, Star."

"Hera, that's the oddest romantic stuff I've ever heard, and I'm only seventeen."

"What, Star? How many other boyfriends do you have that I should know about?"

"Ha-ha, they're all dead."

"Ha-ha oh!"

"Look, Star, cat thirty yards out."

"No, Hera, I say about thirty meters from us."

"Hey, cat! Hey, kitty, kitty."

"Hey, I think you got his attention, Hera."

The cat slowly turned in Hera and Star's direction. Hera flicked his joint and readjusted his bug shield.

"*Madre de Dios*. Zombie kitty. Run, Star, run."

"Oh, shit, it's running toward us, Hera!"

"It's right behind us, Star. Don't look back. Just run."

T' nian Channel, October 15, 3577, 1553 Hours

"Star, wake up. We're almost there. T' ne is just over the channel."

"Why are we descending, Hera?"

"I just called my father. There's a large group of survivors huddling at the pier and not enough boats. He's sending a ferry and personnel and asked for us to give them a hand with the folks." Hera landed the fighter in a large group of survivors. He quickly powered down the bird and hopped out. "People of the apocalypse, apocalypittes, apocalypinese, whatever, I just got ahold of T' ne, and they are sending most boats. So I ask you to chill out for just a couple more minutes and listen to the T' nian personnel."

"Hey, Hera, took ya long enough!"

"Who the fuck said that? I will murder you!" Hera looked into the crowd to see Kimberly and Yonin standing near the fighter. "What the hell y'all doing here?"

"Well, Hera, after helping you and Star at the hospital, I decided I liked you both and wanted to come to T' ne. I heard it was beautiful during autumn," Yonin said.

Hera jumped down and shook Yonin's hand. "Glad to have ya, Yonin. What about you, Kimberly?"

"Howard wants a person from Hotel City to act as a liaison in T' ne and keep the city in y'alls interest."

"Sweet turbo hooah, I like it. I got a crew now." Everyone buckled under a massive explosion in the distance. What in science-green Ad' Drin was that?" asked Hera. Hera and Yonin started to sniff the air. Hera looked at Star and Kimberly.

"Mutants—a lot of them, or maybe one large one. Kind of smells like the aliens we encountered before."

"Everyone, get in the boats now. Fuck the ferry. The ones who can't go, prepare to defend yourself. Everyone, line up against the cars. Star, you ready for one more battle before our vacation?"

"For you, Hera, I'll fight to the end. I just want a shower when this is all said and done."

"That's my girl. Oh, fuck tits." Hera jumped to

the ground as giant mutant trees burst from the Ad' Drin. Each stalk wiped the air, spraying pus all over Hera and his friends.

"Yucky, zombie semen!"

"We got Warper's." Two large alien beings teleported in front of the crowd, firing long lime-green bursts of plasma into the crowd. "Everyone, if you don't need to be here, get out of the channel!" Hera yelled.

One of the Warper's near Star grabbed a young girl and crushed her in his arms. He then reached for pylons on his back, tossing them into the fleeing survivors. He bent back down and then pylon the young girl. Her body twisted upright and began to attack the crowd. Hera and Yonin threw themselves on top of the nearest Warper, firing their weapons into the pylons on the creature's back.

Hera looked over to his side. Star and Kimberly already subdued the other Warper. "Now for the pylon girl." Hera ran and kicked the girl in the side, sending her flying into the channel. Hera pulled out another joint and took a long drag.

"Hera, really I think this is not the time to get high on us!" Star said.

"Star, I don't know if you realize, but I've been stoned for at least 90 percent of this adventure."

"Really, Hera?"

"The large mutant is coming for us now," Yonin said, turning to Hera and receiving the joint.

"If we go over the channel, the mutant will follow us across. I'm not having that thing follow us to T' ne. Y'all go. I will stay."

"Hera, no, I am not going without you. If you're going to stay, I'm gonna stay with you." Hera embraced Star and kissed her.

"Star, you're going home. T' ne is right there. I've done what I promised. Please don't let these couple of weeks be for nothing."

"Hera, I love you."

"I love you too, Star Cassidy. Maybe someday we can make babies."

Star laughed a bit and returned her eyes to Hera. "You have to come back to me, Hera, all right?"

"Okay. Yonin, get her out of here, please." Hera yawned. "At least I got the fighter." Hera dropped his joint and walked over to the fighter. One of the mutant trees lay on top of the aircraft in ruins. "Fuck, I'm gonna have to do this with my brain now." Hera walked over to a car and popped the hood. The ridite generator was still intact. Hera hooked up his tablet to the generator. "Ready to go, huh?" He removed the generator and placed it into his assault pack. "Oh, look, a hover bike. How fucking lucky of me."

"If I had one of these from the start, this adventure would have been a hell of a lot quicker."

"Where are you going, big guy, over the channel? I think not."

Star gazed over at Hera from her boat. She sat at the edge, looking back into the harbor. She slowly wiped the tear from here eye. "Thank you, Hera. Please come back to me. Please come back."

Hera watched the mutant absorb other smaller mutants to gain mass. He powered up the hover bike. "Looks like a rotting man with mommy and daddy issues, but I know the cure: a tall glass of ass kicking."

Hera watched the large mutant jump into the channel. "My time to go, eh?" Hera accelerated the bike into the channel and opened fire on the mutant. The mutant turned his direction toward Hera, sailing down the channel toward it.

Hera raised the hover bike higher toward the large mutant body. "You only live once, huh? Then you go to hell."

Star began to cry uncontrollably now as she watched the large mutant ignite into a large red explosion. "Hera, no! Please, no. I can't believe he's gone. He can't be."

Kimberly threw her arms around Star in comfort. "We are almost home, Star. We are almost home."

Yonin looked into the harbor and squinted his eyes in the afternoon sun. "There's someone in the water. I'm turning the boat around."

"Who is in the water?" Star shot up and looked in the person's direction. The person lazily swam toward them.

"It's Hera! It's Hera!" Star yelled over the boat engine.

"Come and get me, you fuckers. I'm all wet and shit."

Yonin threw the boat right up to Hera so Kimberly and Star could pull him out.

"Fuck, water is everywhere. I'm all wet." Star hugged Hera tightly for a good second. "Ouch! I'm hurting from the explosion. Be careful, Hun."

"Sorry, Hera, I'm glad you're alive."

"Do you have any drugs, Kimberly? I got mine all wet."

"No, Hera, I'm currently out at the moment."

"Good for you. Drugs are bad, kids, really bad."

"How did you survive the explosion, Hera?" Kimberly asked.

"Oh, that. I fell off the bike at the last second."

"You fell off the bloody bike, Hera? They come with seat beats."

"Well, lucky for us, if I used the seat belt, I wouldn't be here today. I just fell off when I hit the accelerator."

"Fell off."

"Fell off like a boss."

"Hey, guys, we are here." Yonin rammed the boat onto T' nian shores. Everyone else made it across the channel and were being greet by T' nian personnel.

People began to yell and argue when they heard about being quarantined. "Hey, I have to do something to calm these people down." He grabbed a microphone from one of the soldiers.

"If you allow me, sir?"

"Go right ahead, kid!"

"Hey, excuse me. Hey, y'all, can I have your attention? I said shut the fuck up!"

"Who the hell are you?" the people in the crowd began to yell.

"My name is Hera Kila' Ka, and I'm the son of the man who owns this island archipelago, but that's of no importance. T' ne is a fresh start for everyone. You all just survived an apocalypse and need to keep on doing so. This island is not just my dad's. It's everyone's. Every single one of you will get land, a house, a new life, and a clean slate, so take what you want or head back across the channel."

Hera threw down the microphone and walked over to Star. "Come on, let's go get our shower, Star." Hera and the others began to walk off.

They were greeted by a middle-aged man who was the same height as Hera and with the same jet-black hair. "Welcome home, Hera."

"Dad, good to be home."

"Are these your friends, Hera?"

"Yes, Dad. Star, Kimberly, Yonin."

"Hmm, I'm going to need a bigger house." All began to laugh at Hera's father's remark.

"Do Mom and Su know I'm home yet?"

"No, not yet, son. I want it to be a surprise for them. Let's go. They are starting dinner."

"Good, I think I have the munchies. Swimming makes me so hungry."

Kila' Ka City, T' nian Isle, January 23, 3578, 1810 Hours

Star looked over the horizon, and the sun fell. Lulis rose over the horizon. She pulled at the dress Hera's father made as a gift. She turned back around to see Hera, Yonin, and Kimberly instructing people in a formation. She turned as Hera ran onto the pier.

"You might not want to stand too close to the water's edge. A mutant whale might snatch you up, Star."

"I am careful, babe. You know I am. Have you thought of a name for the military company, Hera?"

"TPMC T' ne's Private Military Company. I know you said you would be active in the company, as well as you saying you don't want to go back out there in the mainland. But we are gonna make you a section in time. You'll be in charge of your own men. We want you to be the head of training when we are not here."

"Well, I have a lot to learn, huh? I can do it."

"Is there something wrong, Star?" Hera drew Star closer.

"I keep having the same dream that I never left the waste, which I'm still out there on my own."

"This is much for us to take in, Hera. We are kids, and now you want us to save the world. That's a tall order, Hera, really tall."

"The aliens are showing their faces more and more. Now appearances are happening everywhere. Villages and camps are disappearing at an alarming

97

rate. If we don't do something, Star, who will? We alone have the power to make a difference."

"My dream. When I'm alone, I keep asking myself, Hera, what do I do now?"

Hera threw his arm around Star's waist. He placed his hand on Star's stomach. "What do we do now? We survive, if not for us, for those to come, because in the end that's all we can do!"

The moral of the story is don't do drugs in the midst of an alien invasion.

€PILOGUE

So if we are going to fade into dust it will have to be on our own accord. Not by the hands of others or yourselves giving up. Hera, Star, Kimberly and Yonin have just taken in a lot of responsibility in choosing to survive.

Many questions will be answered but many more will deepen the mystery of the unknown invaders and their purpose. And the purpose of the human species Simians. We always want a reason why we are here or where we are going.

It might be more simple then that, just a mistake not anything special. But Hera and his friends will embark on that journey to answer all life questions even the one why we are here. And why they are the only ones to fight these Zombic life forms.